OATH KEEPER

a Hood Academy novel

SHELLEY WILSON

H2O

LIVONIA, MICHIGAN

Edited by Susan Cunningham
Proofread by Ashley Hannen

OATH KEEPER

Published by BHC Press
under the H2O imprint

Library of Congress Control Number:
2017933756

ISBN Numbers:
Softcover: 978-1-947727-39-7
Ebook: 978-1-948540-32-2

Visit the publisher at: www.bhcpress.com

ALSO BY
SHELLEY WILSON

HOOD ACADEMY

Oath Keeper

The Guardians

Guardians of the Dead
Guardians of the Sky
Guardians of the Lost Lands

NON-FICTION TITLES

How I Changed My Life in a Year
Meditation for Beginners
Vision Boards for Beginners
Motivate Me! Oracle Guidebook

ANTHOLOGIES

In Creeps The Night: An Anthology
Featuring "The House On The Hill"
by S.L. Wilson

For Mum

*The monster was the
best friend I ever had.*

~ Boris Karloff ~

PROLOGUE

Previously in Oath Breaker...

Turning my back on one life and stepping into another was terrifying. It's hard to walk away from your friends and family especially when they understand what a messed-up life you lead.

I'm the daughter of a werewolf who was killed by a man who turned out to be my biological father. Left behind by my brother, Zak, who is alpha to the Ravenshood pack, and raised by Frank, a man who knew I wasn't his daughter and made me pay for that every single day. It doesn't get crazier than that.

Witnessing a wolf ripping out Frank's throat, and being whisked away to a school for werewolf hunters by Sebastian, my uncle turned biological dad, is a relatively normal day in the life of Mia Roberts. I discovered a destiny that stretches the realms of sanity. Me: a hunter trained to destroy the wolves. Me: a potential werewolf. Me: capable of love, friendship, loyalty, and strength.

Who knew.

MAKING FRIENDS HAD never been easy for me, but Elizabeth, the bubbly blonde, never gave me a chance to reject her when I found myself dumped in our shared room at Hood Academy, the notorious school for werewolf hunters.

We formed a lasting friendship as we fought off school bullies, freed a tortured werewolf, and pretty much brought about the destruction of the country's oldest establishment.

Over time I learned that Sebastian was trying to keep me safe and build a future for me, but underneath that façade he had another agenda. His one weakness was Mr Parker, the father of my nemesis, Felicity, a redheaded student with a fiery temper and a vicious tongue.

It was Parker who blackmailed Sebastian into producing a cure for lycanthropy: a series of experiments that cost my mum her life. Just before my daring escape from the academy, Sebastian was ready to do a set of tests on me to find out what DNA I had. At the time I'd been horrified, but now, after so many months and still no sign of a fang or claw I half wished he'd managed to complete the test.

Finding out I was descended from a werewolf pack had almost tipped me over the edge. I checked for any sign of advanced hair growth each time I walked past a mirror. Part of me laughed it off as ridiculous, but I couldn't deny that I'd always felt different.

On the flip side, I was also descended from a hunter and for a brief moment, I experienced the honour of accepting the oath in front of my peers. To every pack, a cub is born. Unleash the hunter to protect and serve.

That euphoria hadn't lasted long as Elizabeth and I uncovered the gruesome truth about Hood Academy and the scientific experiments done on the wolves in the secret labs beneath the school building. Our teacher, Miss Ross helped us reveal the truth about Sebastian's experiments.

SHELLEY WILSON

The day I left, Sebastian and I had faced off on the back lawn. He was desperate to keep me at Hood Academy and find out if my DNA was predominantly hunter or wolf. At the time he hadn't cared about the methods he used, waving a gun around and screaming at me to stay. He'd appeared deranged in the pale moonlight. Miss Ross had allowed me to escape by pointing a shotgun at my dad's head, a brave move considering he was her boss and friend.

It sounds like a ridiculous scenario, but Sebastian went crazy; he threatened to kill his own daughter, tore the school apart looking for werewolves, and put the students' lives in danger. Miss Ross stepped up and took over, demonstrating her strength of character and loyalty to both me and my late mother, and also allowing me the time to melt into the woods and begin the life I had wished for since I was a little girl, to reunite with Zak and to become a member of my brother's werewolf pack.

It was only now that I was beginning to understand the saying 'be careful what you wish for.'

ONE

trickle of sweat trailed down the side of my temple, and I swiped at it with a trembling hand. I wished the tremors in my limbs could be blamed on the unusually balmy weather conditions, but they couldn't. I was being hunted, and every part of my body screamed at me to run.

The bulbous moon shone overhead disappearing from view momentarily as the clouds drifted across the sky. The night was warm and muggy, the heat of the summer sun still clinging to everything in its path.

A breeze ruffled the canopy of leaves above, and I held my stance until the rustling subsided. Cody had told me to move in the shadows and to *be* the silence, whatever the hell that meant. He wanted me to become one with nature, to be able to see the ebb and flow of wind currents and smell out the danger. Of course, my gorgeous boyfriend had the advantage of being a werewolf with super-strength and an inbuilt satnav for all things nocturnal. I, on the other hand, was still only a human.

With my seventeenth birthday one month away, it was looking less likely that I had inherited the werewolf genes carried by my mother and brother. Instead, I seemed to be destined to follow my father's hunter line.

My mind wandered briefly to Sebastian. The last time I'd seen him, he was pointing a gun at my head. Not the most fatherly thing to do. Only a few hours ago I'd tried, yet again, to communicate my feelings in a letter to him. The words flashed through my mind as I picked my way through the forest.

Dear ~~Dad~~ Sebastian,

I'm disappointed with the way we left things, and I hope you don't hate me for walking away. Finding out we were father and daughter was a shock for both of us and I don't blame you for how it all turned out, but I need to explain my side of the story. I want you to know how I feel.

You were there for my mother when she needed you the most. You told me how much you cared for her and the evidence I've seen proves just how much she loved you in return, but ultimately it was you who killed her. I'm not sure I can forgive you for that just yet.

Developing your cure for lycanthropy has taken over your entire soul, Sebastian. I can't deny you were trying to help Mum break free from the pack and live a human life, but your frustrations over the flawed serums clouded your judgement and I don't think you realised the damage you were doing.

You began to see me as a second chance, as redemption for her death. By saving me from the fate of the wolves, you would cleanse your guilt. I'm sorry, but it doesn't work like that. I hope you'll recognise why I couldn't let you use me as another lab rat.

I might be a wolf like my mother, or I could be a hunter like you. Either way, I want to discover this on my own. I need space to reconnect with my brother and be a family again.

One day I'd like to return to you so we can try and build a friendship. We've both lost so much. Mum died without telling either of us we were blood relatives, and even your brother was murdered for his part in the horror of my childhood. None of you were there for me, and because of that, I kept you at arm's length.

Trust is something that develops over time, and unfortunately, there have been far too many lies between us. Maybe one day we'll find that bond that every family has. Maybe.

Mia x

I'd reread the words I'd written over and over. They felt forced, almost clinical. It had been Zak's idea to send Sebastian a letter, but the more I stared at it, the more I hated the thought of him reading my innermost feelings.

I didn't hate Sebastian, despite him locking me up and waving a gun at my head. He was my flesh and blood after all and surely if I wanted to be the better person I could offer him some pity.

I rolled my eyes to the sky. Why did any of them deserve anything? My mum had lied about her relationships, died, and left me in the care of a drunk who knew I wasn't his flesh and blood and who punished me relentlessly for it. My beloved brother, Zak, abandoned me to follow his werewolf destiny with the promise of returning to collect me. He didn't. I ended up figuring it all out on my own, as usual. I'd been subjected to abuse for years because of a secret I didn't know.

None of them deserved my pity, or the energy I expended thinking about them. I snatched the letter from the desk and screwed it up, throwing it into the overflowing waste bin in the corner of my room. The blank notepad mocked me as I stormed out, slamming the door behind me.

It had taken me a long time to find any peace in the whirling mess of my brain, but with help from my friends, I was beginning to carve out a life of my own.

The sound of a twig snapping jolted me back to the present, and I gripped the wooden staff I was holding until my knuckles turned white. I sniffed the air just as Cody taught me but all I could smell was the earthy scent of the forest. Then, just as I was about to move forward, I caught a whiff of something else—lavender. Not the soft, subtle kind but a chemical alternative. It was faint but stood out against the aromas of the trees, moss, and leaves. I crouched low and tuned my senses into my surroundings. There were no birds chirping at this time of night, only the nocturnal hoot of an owl and the rummaging of ground feeders. I slowed my pulse and listened. Behind me and to the right I heard the faint sound of breathing. It was a slow and steady rhythm that was almost hypnotic. They'd found me, and I now had two options: stay and fight, or run.

A feral grin spread across my face as I squeezed the staff in my hands and prepared myself to attack. The sound of a soft exhalation filled the space alongside me, and from my hiding spot in the dark undergrowth I raised my eyes to glance at my prey.

In one fluid movement, I lifted from the ground and thrust my staff out so that it swung in the path of the enemy, clipping them full across the chest and flooring them. A yelp followed by a light scream halted my attack.

'Ohmigod, Mia, that hurt!' Elizabeth's bright blue eyes shone in the moonlight as she peered up at me from her position on the floor. Covered in brambles and moss she pushed herself to a sitting position.

'Lavender! Really. There was no other shower gel option for you to choose?'

She giggled, and her entire face lit up.

'I was in a rush, and the lavender one was on special offer.'

'Well, if I *were* a werewolf you'd be dinner by now because your granny-scented soap is stinking up the entire forest. That and the fact you're wearing the brightest pink jumper I've ever seen.'

I extended my hand and helped my best friend to her feet. She grinned at me, zipping up her black jacket to hide the cerise jumper, before launching in for a big hug.

'I've missed you,' she said, squeezing me harder as if to confirm her words.

'I know. I've missed you too.'

'So, you caught me,' she said taking a step back. 'Which makes three to the wannabe werewolf and two to the hunter-in-training.'

Elizabeth dusted herself down as I sniggered at the score. We had spent the last few weeks hunting one another in the forest as part of a secret training pact. In our world, hunters and werewolves didn't mix, but I believed we could flaunt the rules. She was, technically, still a student at Hood Academy, and I was, well, I wasn't sure what I was. There was no way I could return to the academy even if it turned out I did have hunter's blood flowing through my veins. From what Elizabeth had told me, my dear old dad, Sebastian, had vanished without a trace and my nemesis, Felicity, who had made my school life hell, had been parading around school with her evil father, Mr Parker, who was stepping into the role of the headmaster to replace Sebastian.

'Has there been any news from Sebastian?' I'd told myself I wouldn't keep asking Elizabeth for information, but a small part of me just wanted to know that he was safe. He'd appeared broken when we had our standoff on the school lawn right before I left to follow the pack. He'd also resembled a psychotic freak, but under the circumstances, I was willing to forget that. I simply wanted to know that Parker hadn't hurt him.

Elizabeth shook her head. 'Miss Ross has tried everything to get in touch with him, but his phone keeps ringing out. She even tried asking for help from the Governors' Agency, but they refused her request on the grounds of some ongoing investigation they're doing.'

'What's the Governors' Agency?'

'They're the ruling authority over all the hunter academies in the UK. They set the curriculum, hire the staff, and enforce the hunter oath.'

'Ah, you mean the hunters' oath I broke when I ran off with the local werewolf pack.'

'That's the one!'

I laughed, but it felt hollow. In truth, I'd never fully committed to the hunters' oath, merely taking it as part of the façade that I was a normal student. It seemed that the original meaning of the oath had been lost, and the academy had become a corrupt establishment for powerful men to bend the rules and establish their own laws.

'I don't know if I'm supposed to tell you,' Elizabeth interrupted my musings, 'but Miss Ross was sacked today. She was escorted off the premises this morning.'

I wasn't surprised. Miss Ross had helped me escape. Parker wouldn't have thanked her for that, and as he's also Felicity's father, he was always going to be my enemy.

'I'm sure she'll stay in touch.' There was no way Miss Ross would go quietly; it wasn't in her nature. She would find a way to keep in contact with Elizabeth, and I was almost certain she would stay in touch with Zak. She wouldn't just melt into the background, of that I was sure.

'Perhaps she'll head to the Cornwall academy and join forces with Adam.'

Elizabeth's face lit up at the mention of her boyfriend. Following Sebastian's disappearance, it had taken Parker only two days before he transferred Adam to the sister academy in the south, ripping him from Elizabeth's arms. Now, with Miss Ross's dismissal, he'd managed to divide and conquer our little group again.

'I better get back before I'm missed.' Elizabeth hadn't been assigned another roommate after my exit and so sneaking out for our secret training sessions was relatively easy. However, Felicity and her goons were no doubt keeping an eye on Lizzie's movements to see if she could lead them to the pack. Our sessions had to, therefore, involve us hunting one another in the forest, then having a brief catch-up if it was safe, before parting ways.

'I wish you could stay with me at the Mills house,' I said as we strolled in the direction of the academy. 'It's full of boys, and I'm totally outnumbered.'

Elizabeth threw her head back and laughed. 'Oh, and I'm sure the fact that one of those boys is your gorgeous werewolf boyfriend is such a hardship.'

I thumped her playfully on the arm and grinned.

'Having Cody around all the time is the *only* bonus to living on the Mills farm, although I'm not sure Zak is 100 percent happy with Cody and me being a couple.'

'Why? Has he said something?'

'Not in so many words, he just has this look about him when we're together. And, if there's an errand to run he always sends Cody as if he's trying to keep us apart.'

'I'm sure he's just trying to be a responsible big brother, or an overprotective alpha. Either way, it can't be easy to suddenly get his little sister back and find out she's grown into a beautiful woman. You were six the last time he saw you.'

'Yeah, I know. I just wish he'd talk to me about stuff. Since we were reunited, I've been lucky enough to spend all of five minutes alone with him. I miss him more now that he's here than I did when I didn't know where he was!'

Elizabeth giggled and squeezed my hand in her usual supportive manner. I missed having her around all the time too and hated it when we had to go back to our own lives.

The edge of the treeline loomed, and I could make out a couple of lights in the academy. The great expanse of lawn stretched out in front of us as I turned to face my friend.

'Stay safe,' I said, 'and keep away from Felicity.'

'I always do.'

We hugged, and I watched her drop into a low run and sprint across the grass towards the back of the building. She'd have a ladder waiting at the window ready to climb up to our old room, the same ladder Adam used to use when he snuck in for his visits with my friend. That carefree teenage life seemed such a long time ago. I knew that Elizabeth was still in contact with Adam and I kicked myself for not asking about him; after all, he was my friend too.

I turned towards the woods and was about to leave when I spotted two figures running around the side of the academy building toward the old animal cages. An involuntary shudder skittered down my spine as I recalled Felicity locking me up in one of those cages. Instinct told me to return to the pack and report what I'd seen, but I overruled all common sense and decided to follow. Keeping well within the shadows of the trees, I circled the grounds until I reached the dusty trail leading to the cages. I gripped my staff and edged closer, listening to all the sounds that echoed in the night.

From my vantage point in the undergrowth, I could see two students, both friends of Felicity, poking at something inside a cage. No sound came from within: no whimpers, growls, or sobs, and from this angle, I couldn't see what it was. I crept closer.

'I'm glad Mr Parker's using the cages again,' said the first girl. 'This lot don't deserve to be inside the school. Imagine if this thing got out; it could kill us all in our sleep.'

The second student snorted. 'It couldn't hurt a fly. It's weak and useless, but that doesn't matter, 'cause soon it'll be dead.'

The two girls laughed before dropping the prod they'd been using and slinking off in the direction of the back door. I waited. When I believed it was safe enough, I left the sanctuary of the trees and stepped up to the cages. Peering into the inky blackness I thought for a moment that the girls were drunk and had imagined whatever they saw, but then a faint movement caught my eye.

A young girl, no more than ten years old, shuffled to the bars. Her face was covered in dirt and grime, her hair matted to her head. Full, wide eyes gleamed in the moonlight.

'What's your name?' I asked, bending down so I was level with her.

'Arianna,' she whispered, 'but my friends call me Ari. Are you going to rescue me?'

I glanced around the clearing outside the cages, and my eyes fell on the long metal prod the girls had used to taunt Ari. I snatched it up and motioned for the youngster to move away from the bars. Using all my strength, I smashed at the lock until it broke apart and fell to the ground. The door swung open, and Ari emerged sniffing the air.

'Come on!' I reached for her hand and pulled her to the safety of the treeline. We ran hand in hand as deep into the forest as we could before I needed to stop for breath. I collapsed onto a fallen tree trunk and coughed until I thought a lung might pop out. All this training and yet long-distance running was still a weak point for me.

Ari, on the other hand, looked incredibly composed as she perched on the edge of the trunk watching me splutter and choke.

'Do you live around here?' I wheezed.

'No, we come from Yorkshire, but when Daddy needed to visit this area, we all came with him. I got separated from them in town, and then two girls snatched me and threw me in that cage.'

I shook my head. Cody told me when I first arrived how he'd witnessed students from the academy antagonising members of the public but kidnapping a young child from her family was a new low.

'Why did they take you?'

Ari shook her head, her long hair swishing around her shoulders. 'Maybe because I'm a werewolf and they don't like my kind.'

I was stunned. Over the past few months, I'd tried to learn as much as I could about werewolves and nowhere did it say anyone turned before their sixteenth birthday.

'How is that possible? You're so young.'

'Daddy volunteered for my sister and me to have a new treatment. A doctor in a long white coat came to visit our pack leader. He told him about a cure. He said it was safe and that *if* we had the wolf gene, it meant we would never turn.' She kicked at a rock at her feet as she processed the memory. 'It didn't stop us turning, but instead, it speeded up the process. Daddy said we were probably the youngest werewolves in history.' She puffed her chest out and squared her jaw, but that pride didn't reach her eyes.

I licked my dry lips as I processed Ari's words. The treatment she spoke of sounded too similar to be anything but Sebastian's serum, but it was never completed, never finalised, and certainly never administered among the wolf community.

'What did the man in the white coat look like?' I held my breath waiting for Ari to describe Sebastian. I was surprised at the relief I felt at her answer.

'He was short and bald with a funny moustache,' she said. 'And there was a blue picture on the pocket of his coat.'

SHELLEY WILSON

'What did he do to you?' I wasn't sure I wanted to know, if it was anything like the photographic evidence of Sebastian's lab when it was in action. The horrific image of a man chained to a table was forever stamped on my mind.

'The doctor injected us with something and then kept checking our temperature and stuff. We got ice cream for being so good.'

I huffed at the twinkle in her eye when she remembered the ice cream.

The light in Ari's eyes went out, and she dropped her head, wringing her hands together.

'My sister got really poorly and was sick, even the ice cream didn't help. They took her away to try and help her, but we never saw her again. I turned for the first time on the same day.'

A shiver ran down my spine at her words. Was it a coincidence that this doctor promised the exact thing Sebastian had tried to create? Or had Parker found another doctor to replace my father? I was suddenly filled with dread over Sebastian's whereabouts. His serum had been faulty. What if someone had decided to use it despite the fact that it hadn't been stabilised? Could Parker be behind this?

'Where are your parents now?'

Ari lifted her chin and sniffed the air for a few seconds.

'That way.' She pointed in the direction of the Mills family farm. My home.

'You said your father was visiting the area, who did he come to see?'

'He wants to see the alpha. The nasty doctor is visiting all the packs, and bad things are happening to our friends.'

'You mean other people have died as well as your sister?'

'Yes,' she said nodding her tiny head. 'Hundreds of us.'

TWO

It was well into the early hours of the morning when we got back to the farm and, as usual, Cody was nowhere to be seen. The Mills Family Farm truck was missing from the driveway, and I noticed a delivery note pinned to the kitchen door that confirmed he was transporting the farm's produce to a shop over a hundred miles away. The constantly energetic Byron always accompanied Cody on deliveries so at least the house would be quieter without them.

When I'd emerged from the forest after leaving Hood Academy, I experienced a feeling of contentment upon seeing this farmhouse. It was like something from a picture postcard. Redbrick walls and a grey slate roof with a low white fence wrapping itself around the rose-filled garden. I hadn't exactly given much thought to leaving the sanctuary of a school environment and moving in with werewolves.

That had been three months ago and the joy of being reunited with my brother, and being near my boyfriend, was wearing thin. Boys were loud, messy, and disorganised. The farmhouse always resembled the aftermath of a tsunami. Cody's sisters, who were also part of the werewolf pack, had both moved out to live with their own boyfriends. With Zak's blessing, they had joined other packs and lived in cosy little studio apartments nearer to town. I'd wished them well when they left but secretly harboured an intense jealousy that they were getting away from the smell of wet dog and aftershave.

I kicked the pile of shoes to the side as I steered Ari in through the kitchen door. The large black Aga dominated one side of the kitchen and warmed the stone room to a comfortable temperature. Family photographs in mismatched frames covered the furthest wall, and a picture window looked out over the driveway. In the centre of the room stood an enormous oak table with an assortment of chairs dotted around it. Zak sat at the head of the table with his back to the window and a thin man with a closely shaved beard and greying hair perched on a stool to his right. They had their heads bent together in conversation and didn't see us enter.

'Papa!' Ari released my hand and shot into the embrace of Zak's companion. From the other room I heard the cry of a woman, and then Terry burst through the door with a lady close behind him.

'Arianna, oh my baby girl.'

The small family hugged one another, peppering Ari with kisses as tears of joy and relief slid down their faces and I couldn't stop the tug of a smile as I watched the reunion. It wasn't that long ago that I was hugging Zak that tightly after ten years apart. My gaze drifted to my brother who was studying me in return.

'How did you find her?' Zak asked me, his expression not reflecting the joy of the moment.

Ari broke away from her parents and skipped back to my side.

'Mia rescued me from the bad girls at the academy.'

Zak raised a questioning eyebrow and I waved my hand in a non-committal way trying to play down my part in the daring rescue. Ari, however, wasn't going to let it go.

'She burst out of the trees and smashed the lock on the cage and then we ran away.' The youngster gazed up at me with those wide eyes, and I couldn't help but smile.

'I wouldn't exactly use the word burst, Ari. It was more of a slink.'

I felt my cheeks redden as Ari's parents rushed forward with their offer of praise. Terry chuckled from his position behind me as he watched my awkward acceptance of their hugs and well wishes.

'I think it's best if you all try and get some rest.' Zak's voice boomed with authority. 'You can stay in my room, and we'll talk again when the sun comes up.'

Ari and her parents followed Terry as he guided them through to the stairwell and up to Zak's spacious bedroom. I made to follow in the hope I could escape without a reprimand, but I wasn't fast enough.

'Mia, wait!'

My shoulders slumped as I spun on my heel to look at my brother. He was standing now, his big hands placed side by side on the tabletop. His head hung down as he studied something in front of him. I waited without saying a word, something I'd learned to do over the last few months. Zak had his own ways of dealing with the pack, but he had a unique way of dealing with me, almost like he thought I might break.

'What were you doing at the academy?'

'I wasn't technically *at* the academy, I was training in the woods and didn't realise how close I'd wandered to the school grounds, but if I hadn't then I wouldn't have been able to help Ari.'

Silence. Zak didn't move but continued to stare at the paper in front of him.

'I don't want you going out at night any more, Mia.'

'What! No way! How am I supposed to train properly if I can't get my bearings in the woods at night?' I adopted my what-the-hell stance placing my hands on my hips, a deep frown etched across my forehead. How did this keep happening to me? First Frank had abused me and kept me as a prisoner in my own home, then Sebastian locked me in a hospital cell, and now my brother, who I thought would be different, was trying to control me too.

'If you got caught by the hunters I'd never forgive myself. This is the only way I can keep you safe.'

'No! I'm sorry, Zak, but I'm not going to let you treat me the same way everyone else has in the past. I'm not a little kid like Ari, I'm potentially a werewolf like you, and I want to be ready when the change happens.'

Zak's eyes clouded over, and for the first time, I realised he doubted that I had inherited the werewolf gene. It was like a slap in the face. Was that why he was always trying to keep Cody and me apart? He didn't think I was truly one of them?

Terry returned to the kitchen and slung his arm across my shoulder.

'I can train her,' he said giving me a squeeze. 'She should be able to protect herself, no matter what.' He trailed off, and I examined his face. That same expression, the clouded eyes and uncertainty. I wriggled free and slapped his arm away.

'You don't think I'm going to turn, do you?' I wasn't looking for them to answer the question because it was clearly written across both boys' faces.

'Well, screw you,' I shouted. 'Screw both of you.' I stormed out of the kitchen and down the long corridor to the farmhouse extension where my room was located. It was basic but comfortable, and I had my own bathroom. I threw myself on the bed and willed myself not to cry. I didn't want them to think I was weak in any way because I wasn't. I'd survived so much, and none of them ever gave me the credit I deserved, except for Cody; he knew what I'd been through, and he knew how resilient I could be.

I sent a quick message to Elizabeth to check that she'd gotten back to the academy safely and filled her in on the Neanderthal antics of my pack. I wanted to arrange another training session for the next night, partly to annoy Zak and partly because I missed my best friend so much. Within seconds I received a reply.

> [Stay away from the academy, Mia. There's something going on. The place is crawling with Governors' Agency agents. I'll message you when I find out more. E x]

I blinked and reread the message. Elizabeth had only told me that night about the Governors' Agency and their involvement in the various academies across the country. Why were they here? Why now? Surely they couldn't have descended so fast after I freed Ari from the cage. No, it had to be something else. Something the alpha needed to know about.

THE LIVING ROOM of the farmhouse was my favourite room. It had an open fire, which was always crackling and alive despite the temperature outside, and a big squishy rug whose pile was so deep you could wiggle your toes in it. There was a huge sofa with faded fabric and worn armrests that was the comfiest seat in the world. Once you snuggled on there you didn't want to move. Dotted around the rest of the room was an assortment of armchairs that the Mills family had collected over the years. The room was warm and homely. It made me feel safe.

Zak was spread out on the sofa with one arm hanging over the edge. He wore shorts and nothing else. His tanned, muscular torso reminded me of how much I'd missed of his life. He'd been sixteen when I'd last seen him, and yet now here he was, a man, and alpha of a werewolf pack.

'Hey, Mia,' he said without even opening his eyes. I didn't think I'd ever get used to the wolves knowing my scent that well.

'Something's going on at Hood Academy,' I said taking a seat in the armchair opposite him. 'Elizabeth sent this message.' I handed him my phone, so he could read it for himself and watched his face scrunch up with concentration and worry. Being alpha must be a huge responsibility, and I wasn't being fair to him.

'I've seen these Governors' Agency agents before. They made life difficult for a pack in Norfolk a few years ago.'

'What happened?'

Zak looked up from the phone, his expression cold. 'They murdered the entire pack.'

My hand flew to my mouth as I gasped. How could they do that? Yes, the pack were werewolves, but they were also human 99 percent of the time. I couldn't speak for other packs across the country, but I knew for certain that Zak's pack never hunted people, or killed in cold blood. They loved nature and living in balance. None of them deserved to be punished for who they were.

'How?' I almost didn't want to know the gory details, but somewhere deep inside me, I had to know.

'As far as we could tell they were poisoned. The local authority covered it up saying it was a leak in the gas line but Terry and Byron saw some of the bodies and they all had puncture wounds around the main artery in their neck. A single needle hole. We think they were all stabbed by a syringe in their sleep.'

My stomach knotted up, and I had to fight the urge to vomit. Those poor people had been murdered in cold blood by a silent weapon.

'Do you think there's a link to the doctor who injected Ari and her sister?'

'Ari's father told me the doctor was a representative from a new pharmaceutical company who were *sympathetic* to the werewolf cause.'

'Sympathetic?'

'The doctor claimed to have a werewolf wife and daughter who had been cured using the product. The alpha bought it and reported back to the pack so they could choose.'

'Choose to let a weirdo experiment on their family?'

'No, choose to cure their children. Prevent them from turning.'

I wondered if Zak ever regretted leaving home and seeking out his werewolf destiny. Our mother had wanted him to see Sebastian before his sixteenth birthday in the hope that he would have completed his miracle cure for lycanthropy before Zak turned, but my brother chose the pack. A bit like I'd done.

'Do you think Sebastian's involved in this?'

'Sebastian is definitely capable of creating a cure, or poison depending on your interpretation, but after hearing what Terry said on the night you escaped, I don't think Sebastian is capable of mass murder. He's crazy, yes, but I don't think he's a cold-blooded killer.'

'You don't have to protect him on my account.'

'I know, but I realise you must be confused about your relationship with him, and I don't want it to come between us.'

I blinked. 'Why would it come between us? You're my brother. Just because we found out we have different dads doesn't make you any less of a brother to me.'

He smiled an exhausted smile. His eyes crinkled slightly, and I felt a tug in my chest. He seemed so young in that moment, and I had to remind myself of the role he played and the responsibility he held for so many lives.

'That's good to hear, Mia.'

The key in the front door broke the spell between us and I heard the low whispers of Byron and Cody returning from their delivery. My mood lightened on hearing Cody's voice, and I jumped from the chair to open the living room door.

In a flash Zak was off the sofa and grabbing my arm, moving my hand away from the door handle. At my puzzled expression he lowered his eyes to the floor.

'I'm sorry, Mia,' he mumbled, 'but I'm going to need Cody to be focused on the pack until we figure out what's going on. I...I don't think you should distract him.'

I yanked my arm from Zak's grasp, unable to hide the hurt and pain I felt at his words. Turning away from him to pull open the door, I stopped myself from calling after Cody and telling him what my stupid brother had said. I stopped myself from screaming to the entire household that apparently I was never allowed to be happy, but I couldn't stop the feral growl as it rose up from somewhere deep in my gut. From the shocked look on Zak's face, it surprised him as much as me.

I stormed off into the darkness of the corridor and back to my room without another sound. If I ever did become a werewolf, the first thing I wanted to do was bite my brother.

I FELT EDGY and out of sorts the next day. Zak's reaction to me being with Cody had not only annoyed me, but it upset me more than I could put into words. How could he think I'd do anything to interfere with pack business? I knew I was sulking, but I didn't care. If it meant all the boys in the house stayed out of my way for the day then I was onto a winner. Perhaps I could tempt Elizabeth to ditch class and meet me in Ravenshood for a hot chocolate at Taylor's Coffee Shop. The idea perked me up, and I burst into the kitchen with a determination to my step.

Any note of positivity was eradicated when I glanced around at the sombre faces sitting at the kitchen table. Zak was at his usual place at the head flanked by Terry and Byron. Cody sat in between Ari's mother and father. There were a few new faces in the mix, men and women I'd never met before, but as my gaze moved to the assembled group, I spotted a familiar face.

'Miss Ross!'

I rushed to embrace my friend, eager to hear her news, but Zak halted my reunion with his booming voice.

'Mia, take a seat, you need to hear this.' He motioned for me to pull up a chair and from the tone of his voice and his demeanour it wasn't going to be in my best interests to ignore his demand.

I squeezed Miss Ross's hand as I took my place beside her, wishing that she could have brought Elizabeth with her too but also feeling elated to see my godmother again. Her eyes were dull and hooded as she stole a look my way and I wondered how hard Mr Parker had been on her before escorting her off Hood Academy grounds.

Zak cut through my muddled thoughts.

'It's come to our attention that the Governors' Agency, or the GA as they like to be known, have taken up residence at Hood Academy while the students are still on summer break. We don't know if this has anything to do with the pharmaceutical company or if it's coincidental, but we all need to be on high alert. As we've seen before, the GA's presence can only mean danger for the local packs.' He paused to make sure he had everyone's attention before carrying on. 'We've received information from a reliable source that a select group of hunters are still on-site at the academy. We know they're working on a top-secret mission but we can't confirm if this is connected with the Governors' Agency.'

'Do you have any more information on the mission?' a broad, muscular man with a shock of red hair asked.

'Not yet, our source was…compromised before they could pass on any further details.'

My mind was a whirling mass of thoughts. I was aware of the giant man talking to my brother and discussing possibilities, but somewhere in my core something didn't feel right. I'd always thought Miss Ross was Zak's reliable source, but she was sitting next to me. So who was their reliable source? What did Zak mean by compromised? I could feel Cody's eyes on me as I wrestled to slot the ideas and musings together in my mind. There was only one other person at the academy who could report to the pack about what was going on and had a vested interest in seeing Mr Parker and Felicity banished—Elizabeth.

I shot out of my seat tipping the chair over as I went.

'Where's Lizzie?'

Miss Ross stood up slowly and put her arm around my shoulders; she moved her hand so she could squeeze my fingers the way Elizabeth always did when she needed to make me feel better. Cody watched my outburst with a pained expression, unable to help, unable to comfort me.

'I'm sorry, Mia,' Zak whispered. 'We'll do anything we can to help her.'

I narrowed my eyes as I tried to process what he was suggesting.

'No, she can't be. I just saw her...' My words sounded muddled.

How had sweet, innocent Elizabeth got herself mixed up with the Governors' Agency?

'Where is she?' My voice didn't sound like it was coming from me. It sounded distant, cold, and detached. Somewhere on the periphery, I could hear Zak talking, but his words weren't penetrating the thick wall of protection I was building around my heart.

'As far as we can see she's been transferred off-site. The agency is holding her on the offence of collaborating with werewolves, which is against the hunters' oath.'

I wriggled free of Miss Ross's embrace and rushed out of the kitchen door and into the garden. The summer sun was rising in the sky, but the warm rays did nothing to thaw the chill that crept along my spine. I bolted for the gate, running into the forest and picking up speed. The wind lifted my hair and the leaves rustled in the trees as I ran, deeper and deeper into the trees. In the distance, Zak called my name, but I kept moving. I didn't want to stop until my lungs burst or my heart gave up. Why had I left Elizabeth behind at that school? Why didn't I insist that she leave the academy and come live with us at the farmhouse?

If anything happened to her, I would raze Hood Academy to the ground.

SHELLEY WILSON

THREE

Tears streamed down my face as I imagined the horrors Elizabeth must be facing at the hands of Parker and the Governors' Agency. Sebastian and his lab rats were bad enough when they tortured captured werewolves, but these guys were hunters who dedicated their lives to annihilating the packs. Elizabeth had been found guilty of collaboration with the enemy. I could only envision what Parker or Felicity would do to my friend.

I stopped to gather my strength and realised I'd run all the way to the lookout point that Cody and I used to meet at when I ran away from Hood Academy. Ravenshood town and valley spread out below me, but I couldn't see the beauty in the view today, I could only see darkness.

Like some cruel instance of déjà vu, I heard a rustling in the undergrowth. A few short months ago, I'd come face to face with four werewolves in this very spot, not knowing at the time that they were my brother and his pack. My heart thundered in my chest as I waited to see what would emerge from the bushes this time.

Ari broke through the treeline carrying a posy of wild-flowers. She grinned when she saw me, and I relaxed my shoulders and uncurled my fists.

'What are you doing out here?'

Ari gawked at the flowers and then back up at me as if I'd asked her the most ridiculous question in the world.

'I wanted to get Mummy a bunch of flowers, but I saw some of those bad girls again, so I decided to go back to the farmhouse.'

My ears pricked up at the mention of the bad girls. Hood Academy students no doubt, but Zak said most of them were on summer break. I had a feeling the select few girls left behind were Felicity's goons.

'Show me.' I turned Ari around and urged her back the way she'd come. We stumbled on the dirt track that the students followed during their training runs; green flags still marked a safe passage through the woods. I huffed as I recalled Felicity moving the flags and throwing me off course on one of our training sessions.

'This way,' Ari said in a hushed voice, pointing towards a crumbling barn. 'They went behind that building.'

I clamped a hand on Ari's shoulder and pushed her gently to the ground. Crouching beside her I put my finger to my lips and urged her to be quiet. She nodded and dropped down lower into the bushes clutching her pretty flowers.

Stay here, I mouthed.

Creeping forward I was able to assess the building. It had once housed hay bales, possibly for horses kept at the academy before it became a school. The wildlife had taken over it now with swallows' nests visible in the roof beams. Ivy grew up one side covering every inch of brick. As I circled the front, I could see where erosion had taken place and the front side had crumbled. It resembled a ruin you'd normally see on castle grounds. The inside was empty apart from an old cartwheel and lots of weeds. There didn't appear to be anything more to the building. I inspected the area to see if there were any other barns where Ari's bad girls could have gone but there were only trees as far as the eye could see. I was about to return to Ari when I smelled something familiar. Lavender. It was faint, but it was there, lingering in the air. My pulse quickened at the thought of Elizabeth being in danger.

A movement caught my eye, and I glanced over to where I left Ari crouching in the bushes. She was waving at me and pointing towards the back of the building. I moved as quickly as I could until I reached her side.

'Look, over there,' she hissed.

I followed the line of her finger and saw a glint of glass in the base of the wall. It looked like a cellar window. Dropping as low as possible, I shuffled ahead until I was alongside the barn. The wall was weather-worn but solid. I inched closer to the glass and lowered myself onto my stomach. It was a tiny window set into the foundations, a small slit of glass covered in dirt, grime, and greenery. I carefully cleared away some of the brambles and using a section of my sleeve rubbed at the dirty glass.

Beneath the inconspicuous barn was a small room set up with trestle tables and boxes. In the centre was a large table littered with drawings and printouts. I could see the backs of two Hood Academy students, both in their training uniform of grey jumpsuits and matching shoes. Another figure stepped out of the shadows, and I jumped away from the window, slapping my hand across my mouth. Sebastian's hair was unkempt and his face unshaven, and he wore a long white lab coat covered in blood. My stomach rolled, and I gulped in great lungfuls of air to calm my nausea. Was that Elizabeth's blood? The thought that my father could harm my best friend was too much to take in.

Voices filled the air, and I frantically scanned the area for Ari to see if she was safe. I couldn't see her anywhere so I prayed that she was nose down in the undergrowth and out of sight. The two academy students sauntered past within inches of where I lay next to the basement window.

'Do you think his serum would have worked?'

'I don't care, the serum was to help the werewolves, so they never had to turn again. I couldn't care less if it helped them or not. We're trained to kick their furry butts and that's all that matters to me.'

'We won't be able to kick anything if this new stuff wipes them out.'

Their laughter carried through the trees as they walked deeper into the forest leaving me reeling at their words. It wasn't bad enough that Sebastian was creating flawed serums that ended up killing innocent people, it now sounded like he was making a weapon to kill *all* werewolves.

Ari appeared above me dragging me out of my stupor.

'I've found the way in.' She motioned for me to follow and I scrambled to my feet dusting off my jeans as I went.

There was a trapdoor hidden under a mound of ivy a few yards away from the old barn. By the look of the well-worn path in the mud around the entrance it was a facility someone used often.

'I saw the bad girls climb out of here.'

'Thanks, Ari. You did really well. Now, do you think you could be the lookout while I go inside?'

Her eyes gleamed with pride as she puffed her chest out and gave a little salute.

'Aye, aye, Captain.'

I smiled at her, pleased that she was by my side no matter how young the little wolf was.

'I'll be back soon.' I hoped that wasn't a lie. I had no idea what I was walking into. The lab beneath the academy had been one long row of single rooms leading off one another, each room holding a fresh horror. Was I about to venture into another evil place filled with test tubes, dusty files, and dried blood?

A ladder balanced against the opening leading down into the darkness. I cursed at not having a torch or weapon with me. When I'd stormed out of the kitchen an hour ago, I hadn't imagined this was how my day would unfold.

Upon reaching the ground, I waited until my eyesight adjusted to the gloom. I was standing in a square space with no way out except the corridor straight ahead. Cut into the wall was a heavy metal door with a small window. I moved forward, tuning into my senses as Cody showed me. The window was made of reinforced glass, which made it difficult to see through or decipher with any real clarity what was inside. However, I saw a man in a white coat moving around the space and assumed this was my deranged father.

The door handle turned with ease, and I pressed my shoulder against the metal and inched it open. Sebastian had his back to me. He was scribbling notes on one of the many pads scattered across the table. The smell of lavender permeated the room, which I scanned for any sign of Elizabeth. To my left was a shelving unit with row upon row of syringes in sterile packaging. Boxes marked with a blue pharmaceutical logo filled the floor space.

So, there was a link between Sebastian and the pharmaceutical company, but was the GA involved too?

The window I'd peered through only moments ago was high in the wall above Sebastian's head casting a dim light over his work. My gaze drifted to the right where two trestle tables were laid with blankets. I'd seen something similar to this in the lab beneath the academy. Sebastian chained the werewolves to the table and injected his serum into their body, gauging the response and recording his findings. Was this where Ari and her sister had been treated? If not, that meant there could be facilities like this one dotted across the country. I couldn't imagine any alpha allowing members of his pack to come here even if there was the hope of a cure for lycanthropy.

41

I allowed my eyes to travel to the furthest corner of the room. There, on the floor of a small metal cage, was Elizabeth's pink jumper, but my friend was nowhere in sight.

The rage that overcame me was swift. My fingers curled up into tight fists, and all I could hear was the blood pumping around my body. The smell of lavender was overpowering, and somewhere I could hear the slow tick of a wristwatch. Before I could stop myself, a deep growl rumbled from my throat. Sebastian spun around clutching the table behind him. His face registered shock and then fear. What did he have to be scared of?

'Mia! How did you find...? What are you doing...?' His eyes shifted to Elizabeth's jumper and realisation dawned.

A roar in my head drowned out everything else in the room. I was aware that Sebastian was trembling. I could smell the fear rolling off him. Every speck of blood and grime on his white coat stood out, and even the clump of grass stuck to his shoe attracted my attention.

'It's okay, Mia. She's okay; no one hurt her, I made sure of it.'

My hands ached where I was clenching them so tightly, and they felt slick. Beads of sweat dripped from between my fingers and hit the floor.

'Mia, I'm so sorry I couldn't help you.' Sebastian held his hands out in a gesture of surrender. 'But I haven't given up on you, I promise. Please trust me when I say I'm looking out for you.'

A guttural sound escaped me as I swept my gaze between the cage and Sebastian. The sweat glistened on his forehead.

'The GA have her, they've taken her for questioning, something about breaking the oath. I...I told them not to harm her.'

I took a step backward and then another until I was in the gloomy corridor. I reached out for the metal door and readied myself to slam it in Sebastian's face, but instead, I stopped in shock. I caught sight of my hand. Huge claws protruded from my fingers, blood dripping from them. I turned my palm over to see the four small puncture wounds where the claws had dug deep into my hand, although it wasn't a human hand any more, it looked part human and part wolf.

Sebastian took a step forward, and I flinched.

'Mia, I can help you. I've finished my work, and we have a cure.'

I shook my head and took another step backward. The roar in my head was still there, but I could also hear Ari moving about in the forest above. What the hell was going on?

'You don't have to do this alone, Mia. I'm your father, and I will always have your best interests at heart. I can save you from this fate.'

I left the door where it was and spun on my heel running for the ladder. I climbed up the rungs in two leaps and slammed the trapdoor shut behind me.

Ari stood a short distance away watching me with wide eyes.

'What?' My words sounded odd like I had too many teeth in my mouth. I lifted my clawed hand and felt around my lips. A bump caused my top lip to protrude. I ran my fingertip down the lump and met something sharp and solid. A fang.

My eyes filled with tears as I processed what was happening. I was turning. This was it. No more feeling like I didn't belong with Cody and my brother, I was finally going to be a proper member of the pack. I was going to be a werewolf, like my mum.

I grinned, and Ari flinched. Clearly a fang-filled mouth wasn't conducive to a pretty smile. Throwing my head back, I laughed; it felt wonderful to finally belong. I stared up at the lush green canopy of leaves, and the blue sky above. I closed my eyes and soaked up the feeling of the warm sun on my skin. Wait a minute. That wasn't right. Where was the full moon?

'Mia, can you hear me?'

I glanced over at the young wolf and noticed she was still keeping her distance. I nodded.

'We need to get out of here.'

That was an understatement. Not only had I proved to my father that I had inherited my mother's werewolf genes, but I'd also shown him that I could half turn in the middle of the day. He'd have a field day dissecting me in his laboratory.

Ari grabbed my hand and pulled me in the direction of the Mills farm. It was a long walk back home, but we seemed to make great time as we sprinted through the trees.

Looking down at my body I noticed I was still a human: two arms, two legs, a human torso. No hairy limbs or cracking bones. I'd watched Cody turn when Felicity attacked him, and it had been horrific. He broke nearly every bone in his body, changing shape until he became a huge wolf the size of a horse. I was still little old me. My hair brushed my shoulders, and when I lifted my clawed hand, I could feel a human nose and cheekbones. What the hell was wrong with me?

WITH THE FARMHOUSE in sight, I slowed to a walking pace. Ari rushed through the back door, and I heard the commotion in the kitchen as the pack listened to the young wolf's expressive account of the morning. I expected Zak to come barrelling out of the door, but I was delighted when Cody emerged.

He spotted me instantly. I heard the gasp like a cannon blast across the sky. The muscle in his cheek twitched as his gaze dragged from the fangs to my clawed hands. Recovering himself, he sauntered over to where I stood, as if this was an everyday occurrence. His eyes never left mine.

'Hey, Mia.'

He gave me that lopsided grin that melted my heart but all I could do was huff. I didn't have a clue how I'd partly changed into whatever the hell I was so I was clueless as to how I changed back to me; to Mia, the human girl.

A tear slid down my cheek. Cody caught it on his thumb and brushed it away. He pulled me into a tight embrace and allowed me to sob into his chest. His scent was safe and comforting, and I melted into him. I reached up to cling to his shirt and noticed my hands were normal, no claws and no deep wounds. I broke out of Cody's embrace and touched my face. No fangs. I was me again.

'You okay?'

I was shaking so much that my voice wobbled when I spoke.

'Yeah, I think so.'

'Want to tell me what happened?'

'I found Sebastian; he's in a storage facility in the woods. I followed Lizzie's scent but found him instead. I lost it. I felt so angry with him, with the academy, and with myself.'

He pulled me close again and whispered into my hair.

'Why are you so angry with yourself?'

'Because I haven't turned, or hadn't, and I didn't think I ever would. Where does that leave me, or us, or me and Zak?'

'You know what I think?'

I shrugged and snuggled into his arms.

'I think you worry too much.'

I laughed and leaned back to look up at him. His blonde hair flopped into his eyes, and I brushed it away with my fingertips. His smile lit up his face, and I felt the ice in my heart begin to melt again. He dipped his head to mine and kissed me gently. All the worry over Sebastian, the academy, my abnormal transformation evaporated as his lips moved over mine.

A small cough behind us broke the magic spell, and we wrenched ourselves apart.

Zak was watching my exchange with Cody with sad eyes. I knew he'd be mad at me for running off and being reckless, and he was probably as confused about my half turn as I was, but part of me didn't have the energy to care. He might be my flesh and blood, but I was still getting to know him. Elizabeth was my family, and I couldn't stand by and do nothing.

'The GA are holding Lizzie for questioning. I'm going to get her back as soon as it's dark.'

I was expecting an argument, or at the very least some resistance from him, but instead, Zak dragged his big hands through his hair and said, 'Okay, but you take Terry and Cody with you.'

He turned to address the assembled pack members. 'If they want a fight, then we're going to give them one.'

He looked every inch the alpha as he took charge and I felt a surge of pride as I watched the assembled group nod their approval.

Cody threaded his fingers into mine, and I relaxed, relishing the warmth of his touch. The heaviness in my chest lifted, and I smiled, feeling calmer and happier than I had in a long while. Finally, I was going to get the opportunity to be a proud member of my brother's pack.

FOUR

Zak pulled my collar up around my neck in an affectionate gesture.

'Watch your back, stay sharp, and let Terry take the lead.'

I nodded, stopping myself from pointing out it was Elizabeth and me who rescued Terry from Hood Academy when Felicity and her goons captured him several months earlier. In Zak's warped world anything I'd done before living under his roof didn't count. I was his little sister, and he wasn't going to let me forget it.

'Ready?' Cody poked his head around the doorframe, a black hat encasing his head camouflaging his brassy blonde hair.

Smiling up at my brother I spun on my heel and followed Cody out into the night.

Terry was waiting for us beyond the garden gate, and several of the pack had gathered to watch us leave. Having them there disturbed me, and part of me wanted to question their reason for congregating. Their furtive glances to one another told me there was something going on that I wasn't a part of.

Before I could ask the question, Cody had herded me out of the gate and off towards the treeline. As we stepped into the dark forest, any worries I had evaporated.

CREEPING AROUND THE grounds of Hood Academy at night brought back a tsunami of thoughts and emotions. It wasn't that long ago that sneaking out after dark was a highlight because it meant a rendezvous with Cody.

My heart soared as I glanced across at my werewolf boyfriend. I had never imagined it would be possible for me to have anyone to share my thoughts with. My home life had resembled a prison, and my brief stay with Sebastian at school had been turbulent at best. Cody was like a solid anchor keeping me safe. After Zak's brotherly outburst I'd worried that my time with Cody was coming to an end. It was my intention, after this night, that Zak would be able to trust in my abilities and understand that Cody and I being together wouldn't affect his precious pack.

'Do you have any idea where they would keep her?' Terry whispered as we reached the black expanse of lawn that backed onto the property.

I had visions of her chained to the same gurney they'd used for Terry down in the bowels of the academy, but a shadow caught my eye and I breathed a sigh of relief.

'She's there.' I pointed at the patio doors that led to Adam's old room. It was apt that they would lock Elizabeth in that room surrounded by memories of her lost love. It was also the same place Terry and I had escaped from before Sebastian chased after us. A shiver skittered down my spine.

'Well, that's handy.' Terry's wide grin made me giggle as I realised he was remembering the same thing. 'Let's hope your dad hasn't been left in charge of the key to the gun cupboard.'

I rolled my eyes and thumped him on the arm, and his warm laugh rumbled from deep in the back of his throat. Se-

SHELLEY WILSON

bastian had shot Terry that night but he recovered quickly thanks to his werewolf healing. I didn't know if I had that ability to heal. I was half a wolf, or a wannabe werewolf as Lizzie liked to call me. If I got shot, I'd probably bleed out and die.

'We'll circle the lawn using the trees for cover. Cody, I want you to keep watch on the perimeter and warn us if anyone approaches.'

Cody nodded and melted into the forest. A warmth spread through my chest at Terry's decision. It would have been much easier to leave me behind in the trees as a lookout, but instead he trusted me to work with him. If only my brother felt the same.

As we approached the back of the academy, I saw Elizabeth through the partially closed curtains. She was sitting on the end of Adam's bed with her head bent forward and her hands bound in her lap. Her slumped posture worried me. Elizabeth had grown over the months we'd known each other. She'd been a sweet and innocent girl who flourished into an accomplished hunter. The girl in that room looked broken and terrified.

I half stood ready to rush towards the patio doors, but Terry was quick to pull me down to my knees.

'Wait! Not yet.' He nodded at the gap in the curtains once more as two men in black trousers and matching jumpers walked in front of the window. The GA. I tuned into my wolf senses and heard the faint rumbling of an authoritative voice.

'It's imperative that you cooperate, miss. This establishment has become a laughing stock and I, for one, will not allow its reputation to remain in ruins. A displaced headmaster, a student running off with the local werewolf pack. Surely you understand why we need to carry out this review.'

Elizabeth nodded, her long blonde hair shielding her face.

'Where did Miss Roberts go? Does Dr Roberts still have contact with her? Why did Mr Parker dismiss Miss Ross? Was she somehow involved? Answer me!'

I could see Elizabeth's shoulders shake as she cried and when she lifted her head my heart almost broke in two. Her eye and cheek were bruised, and she bore a long split across her lip. Eyes puffy from crying, and an ashen face completed the look.

Anger raged through me and it was almost unbearable. I wanted to break down the doors and rip those men apart. As if sensing my rising fury Terry held on to my arm, his warmth seeping through me and calming the roar in my head.

'Be patient, Mia. We're going to get her out of there.'

I believed him. Terry and Elizabeth had bonded when they rescued me from my delusional father, and I knew he cared for her as a true friend does.

'I don't know anything,' Elizabeth was saying. 'I haven't seen Mia since the night she left, or Dr Roberts. I only found out Miss Ross had been sacked when I saw Mr Parker escorting her off the premises. You have to believe me. I don't know anything.' Her voice broke as she sobbed her words.

'Well, we don't believe you. Miss Parker found you snooping in her father's office. Why were you in there? What were you looking for?'

'Felicity is wrong! I wasn't snooping; I was waiting for Mr Parker as I had an appointment with him.'

'Don't lie to me,' the man roared causing Elizabeth to flinch. 'Mr Parker denies that he asked you to his office. He is a respected member of the GA and the new headmaster of this school, and you are nothing. Who do you think we'll believe?'

Elizabeth dropped her head and curled into herself as the man raged on. My mind flashed back to the many times Frank had stood over me like that, his menacing voice the only sound to echo around the small house.

'I've had enough of this idiot,' Terry said with a hard edge to his usually warm voice. 'Stay here.'

I watched as he crept along the building, sticking to the shadows. He skirted past Elizabeth's room and kept going.

SHELLEY WILSON

I wondered what he had planned until I heard the smash of glass from the far end of the school, the rock he had thrown breaking the second story window with ease.

Leaving Elizabeth bound in the chair, the two men left the room as they went to investigate the noise. I heard their heavy breathing mingled with that of others as they all ran through the corridors towards the main staircase.

I rushed forward and kicked at the patio door with all my strength. It smashed open making Elizabeth scream and jump off the bed. The fear on her face evaporated when she saw it was me.

'What have they done to you?' I asked striding to her side and studying the bruises on her face.

'It was Felicity. She tried to get information out of me before handing me over to the GA. Never mind that now, what are *you* doing here?'

'Rescuing you, come on.' I grabbed her elbow, and we fled the room crunching over the broken door and running straight into Terry. Elizabeth screamed again until she spotted Terry's muscular frame. He unravelled her binding and we each grabbed her hands, half running, and half dragging her into the safety of the trees.

Cody was waiting for us as we barrelled through the overhanging boughs and scratched our faces on the tiny branches in our path.

'Four students left the building by the front door and have split up to circle the school,' he told Terry. 'We need to draw them off the girls.'

Terry grunted his agreement and grabbed my shoulder with his big hand.

'Mia, I need you to head back towards the farm as fast as you can. Me and Cody will split up and confuse the hunters so they don't know what direction to go in.'

I gave a short nod of my head and grabbed Elizabeth's clammy hand. She squeezed my fingers, and I smiled at her. It was up to me to get my friend to safety.

We turned and ran, leaving the boys to do what they needed to. We sprinted hand in hand in the direction of the farmhouse, making no sound, until our lungs threatened to burst.

I SLOWED DOWN when I realised Elizabeth was struggling to keep up. I didn't want to ask her what she'd been through. She'd tell me in time.

I closed my eyes and sniffed the air sorting through the scents in my mind: moss, pine, earth, and something else, something that was out of place in this part of the forest. A bittersweet perfume wafted through the trees masking the natural aromas, and the hairs stood up on the back of my neck. I knew that smell; I remembered how it used to make me gag whenever it clawed at my throat in the academy classrooms or the gym changing room. Only one person I knew wore such an overpowering perfume.

My eyes snapped open. Felicity stood in front of us with her staff held out to the side like a broadsword. Her fiery red hair was scraped back into a high ponytail emphasising her sharp cheekbones. She was smirking in that infuriating manner that suggested she'd beaten you already.

'Finally,' she said. 'I've been looking for you all over these woods, Mia. I *really* wanted to thank you for running away.'

I knew she was goading me to get a reaction, but I couldn't help the rush of anger that swept over me.

'I didn't run, Felicity, I was driven away by you and your maniac father.'

She laughed; it was a short, humourless sound.

'The academy is no place for a wolf girl, I told you that.'

A red fog began to descend and settle in my vision, and I took a deep breath to try to control it. The change seemed to be powered by my anger, and I couldn't let Felicity force my shift. I needed to learn to manage my emotions, or the were-wolf gene would dominate my entire personality.

'What's the matter, *wolf girl*? You afraid you'll break a claw or ruffle your fur?'

The blood pumped faster around my system, and I tried in vain to slow the rhythm down.

'I owe you a beating,' Felicity continued. 'It wasn't the same using dear old Elizabeth as a punching bag.'

I pushed Elizabeth behind me to safety as I felt the turn snap into place in my mind. The rage overcame every molecule of my body, and the feral growl rushed up and out startling Felicity with the ferocity of the sound.

Any initial shock at my snarling was quickly pushed aside as a calculated grin spread across Felicity's face. This was what she wanted. For so long she'd only been able to prod and poke at my ancestry, but she'd never had proof that I was indeed a wolf girl. Until now.

'There's my girl,' she hissed.

I was beyond controlling anything now. Felicity had always been able to bring out the wolf in me, even before I knew that was a possibility. I'd flipped during a class training session once and beat her until her nose bled and her eyes were swollen. She believed she owed me a beating in return, but instead of feeling disorientated with my transition I felt powerful, strong, and focused. Felicity was the enemy, and I hunted the enemy.

I squared my shoulders and moved my stance so my feet were shoulder width apart, just as Miss Ross had taught me in my training sessions. Felicity moved her staff in front of her and gripped it in both hands, her eyes never leaving mine.

I flicked my right hand out to the side as if shaking something off it and watched Felicity's eyes shift to scrutinise the sharp claws that snapped into place. I stretched my fingers, curling and uncurling them to test the power in my claws.

My top lip ached as I felt the fangs slide into view cracking my jaw as they manoeuvred into place.

It all happened in a matter of seconds, but it felt like the process was drawn out. Felicity was mesmerised by my shift, her eyes blinking rapidly as she inched back a step and part of me wished that I too could see what I had become. The roar of adrenaline in my head threatened to overwhelm my senses, but I managed to retain a thread of my human self and cling to it. I couldn't risk losing myself totally.

Felicity jabbed forward with her staff and struck me in the chest. I stumbled backward with a grunt but quickly recovered.

'You're pathetic, *wolf girl*. You're not even a proper werewolf.' She laughed at me as she moved across my path. 'You can't even get that right.'

I shook off the goading and concentrated on my prey. I couldn't let her distract me into doing something stupid.

We moved around each other, looking for breaks in defence or a weak spot that could be manipulated. Felicity systematically swung her staff at me like a child would antagonise an ant's nest with a long stick. There was no sense of urgency about her movements. She planned to enjoy hurting me, but I wasn't prepared to give her the satisfaction. I was a member of the pack, and this was my chance to prove how powerful we were by sending Parker a message.

I swiped a clawed hand across the air between us and my nails grazed Felicity's cheek. It was so fast that she didn't see it coming and she yelped, jumping backward, with a trickle of blood running down her face.

'You bitch,' she hissed. 'You'll pay for that.'

In a flurry of movement, she advanced on me whirling her staff around like a cheerleader's baton. It hit me hard on the shoulder, thigh, and side of the head, and my ears rang from the impact.

I retaliated with two fast swipes of my claws, slicing left and right until I felt the softness of her flesh. She screamed out in pain, and I grinned at the sound. Any part of me that was human faded away as I was overtaken by the primal instinct to hunt and kill.

Felicity must have felt the change in me too as she backed away clutching a hand across her stomach to stem the flow of blood.

'My father was right,' she heaved. 'You *all* deserve to die!'

With a warrior's cry she launched herself at me swinging her staff from high above to knock me off balance. I skidded to the floor and winced at the sudden impact. She didn't waste any time and was above me in seconds, wielding her staff and bringing it down repeatedly on my crumpled form.

I felt the pain of each blow although I could also feel my body begin the instantaneous action of healing itself. I marvelled at the capability of my partial werewolf form as the beating rained down on me from above.

Felicity began to tire. Her strikes weren't as brutal yet the blood that clouded my vision and poured down the side of my face told another story.

In the distance I heard Terry and Cody approaching, their huge paws pounding on the compacted earth as they tore through the forest.

I needed to end this before they arrived. I wanted to prove to Zak what a valuable member of the pack I could be. Felicity had to understand that the wolves weren't going to give up their lives without a fight.

Bursting from the dirt floor, I leaped to my feet and howled, a deep guttural sound that shook the branches of the trees close by. Felicity baulked. I took advantage of her confusion and launched myself at her, clamping down on her throat with my fangs. I tasted her blood as it gushed from the wound in her. The gurgling sound of her choking broke through the roaring rage, and I let go. She dropped to the ground gasping for breath and clutching her hands to her throat, her eyes wide with terror.

My face screwed up into a snarl as I crouched low over her trembling body. I traced a claw along the side of her face leaving a tiny trail of blood in its wake. Blood frothed at her mouth as she coughed and sobbed. I felt nothing. No remorse, no anger, just a desire to finish her. I spread my hand wide and uncurled my claws lifting my arm above my head in readiness to strike.

'Mia, no!' Elizabeth's cry was cut short as a golden wolf burst through the bushes and skidded to a halt a few feet away. I recognised Cody's scent immediately.

More wolves followed, a mix of colours: light brown, silver, black, and a dark brown, the latter being twice the size of the other wolves. I sniffed the air and my shoulders sagged as Zak's scent filled the small space. He bared his teeth and growled at me. My entire body shook as I tried to resist his cry. He was my brother, and he was trying to stop me from making a fatal mistake. He was also my alpha, and I couldn't act against him.

Lowering my arm, I backed away from Felicity and stood up to my full height. She stared up at me with pure hatred gleaming in her eyes. Blood poured from her neck wound and dribbled out of her mouth. I had no idea if she would, or could, recover from her wounds and the werewolf part of me didn't care. The human part of me, Mia, was slowly returning and my eyes grew wide as I looked down at my handiwork. My claws began to retract leaving a dull ache in my hands and my mouth felt normal again as my fangs disappeared.

'Leave,' I whispered. 'Before I kill you.'

Felicity scrambled to her feet and ran, tearing through the trees on wobbly legs, using her free hand to try to keep herself upright as she manoeuvred through the forest. I watched her until she disappeared from sight and then I kept watching that space for a long time not wanting to look at my brother, Cody, or the other wolves. What would they think of me? What had I become?

OATH KEEPER

FIVE

I stared at my reflection in the mirror, my eyes flitting from the bruises on my cheek to the cut on my lip. Felicity had given it her all when we fought, throwing all her anger, fear, and training into hurting me. I didn't blame her. I couldn't. She was entitled to hate me for the beating I'd inflicted on her all those months ago and now, well, now she had more cause than ever to want me dead.

Is that how Frank had felt when he beat me? Had he lost all control of himself when he kicked and punched me? Was I no better than the man who raised me under a cloud of terror?

The wolves had dispersed quickly following my altercation with Felicity as they sensed the upcoming battle between their alpha and his little sister—the wannabe werewolf. I couldn't deny it any longer. I wasn't a proper wolf, I wasn't a valid or valuable member of the pack. I was a stupid girl who just so happened to have fangs and claws when someone pissed her off. I was a typical teenager.

Zak led me back to the farm in silence. Cody followed a few steps behind. I had an insane and inappropriate urge to giggle as

I likened the scene to a prisoner being transported to their doom. I was Anne Boleyn!

No one spoke to me or even looked in my direction as I was escorted to my room. I wanted to express my annoyance that Zak hadn't left Lizzie's rescue up to me, Terry, and Cody but felt the need to follow with the entire pack. He'd had that planned all along, which was why they had all congregated when we left earlier. Zak had prepared himself for me screwing it all up.

The door closed behind me, and I only caught the slightest glimpse of Cody, his shoulders slumped and his eyes sad, before the loud clunk of the wood in the frame. I waited for a few moments and then tried the handle. It opened. I closed the door again, but the heavy weight in my chest lifted ever so slightly knowing they hadn't locked me up as Sebastian had.

That girl in the mirror was an imposter. She wasn't who I wanted to become. I'd survived so much in such a short time, and I knew I was stronger for it. I could feel that inner drive spurring me on to be better than the losers who had hurt me. I wasn't going to make the same mistakes, but here I was, banished to my room because I'd let my emotions get the better of me. I didn't know who to turn to for help. Zak was my brother but he was also the alpha; he had to be extra tough on me for the sake of the pack. Cody meant the world to me, but he was a valuable member of Zak's inner circle. Miss Ross and Elizabeth were like my family, but they didn't have the knowledge to figure this out.

There was only one person who could help me. One person who might know what I was becoming and how to handle it.

I closed my eyes and took a deep breath. Was I ready to deal with the devil? Was I so far gone that the only chance I had at finding the real Mia was in the hands of a maniac? I snapped my eyes open again. I saw a coldness there, a lack of empathy, and something else, something deeper and more frightening. I saw rage buried below the surface. Rage at my-self, my mother, Frank, Zak, and Sebastian. If anyone could help me to figure it all out, then it was him. Sebastian could well be my only hope.

THE STARS LIT up the night sky as I sat by the open window. One of the wolves I didn't know delivered my evening meal. Clearly Zak didn't want me talking to my friends, and I couldn't blame him.

I could see the extra cars in the driveway and hear the voices of many visitors drifting up from the kitchen. Packs from all over the country had started to gather, and it was Zak's job to hear their stories and work out a plan of action. I didn't want to cause my brother any more heartache than he was already dealing with but I was also aware that without me in the picture he could concentrate all his efforts on saving the wolves and securing the packs' future.

Yes, he'd be mad, and so would Cody, Elizabeth, and Miss Ross but if I could return to them with answers that might help them rather than hinder them, they couldn't stay mad for long.

I sucked in a breath and slung my backpack over my shoulder, dropping my phone on the bed as I went. If I was go-ing to do this, I couldn't have them contacting me or risk Zak tracing my phone. It was now or never. The warm and musical tones of my family and friends' voices vibrated through the floorboards pulling me in two directions. It would be too easy to slide between the sheets of my bed and wait for everyone else to look after me but I didn't do easy and I didn't do victim. I'd survived more than most girls my age and it was time to stand alone again and fight for what I believed in.

Swinging my legs out on the ledge, I waited until I could train my enhanced hearing onto the sounds from the kitchen.

'Why is the GA here?'

'That doctor has no right to use experimental serums on our children.'

'We don't have all the facts. Elizabeth told us the GA is here to review the academy after recent events. We have no idea if there is any link between them and the pharmaceutical company.'

'Yet our kids are still at risk.'

'It could be a free-for-all. If our kids have that injection they'll either die or they'll turn early. The hunters think they're free to hunt without remorse, killing our children.'

The conversation raged on with voices unknown to me contributing their thoughts. Zak was surprisingly quiet, perhaps taking in all the information and worries before working on a solution. I could hear Terry and Cody adding to the discussion with Terry offering his first-hand account of being held captive at Hood Academy and the many times they'd carried out a rescue.

As quietly as I could, I shimmied down the trellis that ran down the side of the house from my window, dropping lightly to the floor. Crouching for a few moments, I made sure that no-one had heard me but I don't think the assembled packs would have heard a chainsaw over the heated discussion they were having.

Through the cosy glow of the kitchen light, I could see Zak at the head of the table, his brow furrowed as he listened to his friends. Cody stood behind him with Terry and Byron on either side. They had each other, and a small part of me was grateful for the fact that they were so close. Brothers united. Miss Ross would look out for Elizabeth, which only left me – the outsider. It was a role I'd played my entire life, and I slipped into it like an old pair of gloves. Sebastian might be a crazy scientist with more flaws than most human beings but he was also my biological father, and I had to hope and pray that this fact was enough to keep me safe, at least until I learned what I needed to about my genes.

I took one last look at my family and friends before melting into the darkness of the forest, their voices growing fainter with every step I took.

THE EMPTY BARN where I'd found Sebastian stood a short distance away. It was cloaked in shadows and looked as derelict as it was supposed to be. Finding my father in a secret room below the ramshackle building was the only clue I had. No doubt he would have moved, or been moved by whoever was in charge, but I hoped there was enough of his scent left for me to follow.

I climbed down the ladder into the blackness below. It didn't fill me with as much dread as when I'd descended the same steps in the hope of helping my friend. That inevitability that I was about to come face to face with my dad had hijacked the moment. At least this time I had a torch.

The room where I'd found Sebastian was now empty, the tables cleared of all paperwork, and the equipment he'd been using gone, the small imprints in the dust the only sign that he'd been here at all. I swivelled the torch towards the far corner, but the boxes with the pharmaceutical logo had also vanished.

A faint scuffling noise filled the air behind me causing the hairs on the back of my neck to stand up. Goose bumps trailed down my arms as I tuned my senses to the surrounding area and the entrance. If Sebastian was still lurking, maybe I would get a chance to talk to him before he launched into an assault or capture.

I clicked the torch off, plunging the room into darkness, and waited for my eyes to adjust. Sniffing the air, I tried to determine what, or who, I could be about to face. I lifted the torch above my head ready to wallop whoever appeared then I caught the faintest whiff of a familiar scent—lavender.

Elizabeth's pale face shone in the muted light cast by the window high up on the wall as she moved into the doorway. Her eyes were as wide as saucers, and yet I had the overwhelming urge to shout 'Boo!'

Instead, I lowered my makeshift weapon and walked to the centre of the room.

'What the hell are you doing here, Lizzie?'

She jumped at the sound of my voice then her eyes adjusted to the dim light, and she could make out my shape.

'I was worried you'd do something stupid,' she said glancing around the room. 'Like return to the scene of the crime.'

I huffed. It had been a reckless thing to do, but deep in my bones, I knew Sebastian wouldn't be here in person. I just needed to inhale his scent, gather my strength, and push forward.

A rustling behind Elizabeth's back drew my attention, and I almost yelped when a tiny figure darted out of the corridor to join us.

I stared from one face to the other.

'When did you think it was a good idea to bring Ari along?'

Elizabeth rolled her eyes and nudged the child with her elbow.

'See, I told you she wouldn't like it.'

Ari giggled.

'I saw you climb out of your window, so I went to get Lizzie. You're lucky I didn't tell Zak!' She put her tiny hands on her hips and tilted her chin looking every inch the defiant young pup she was.

I couldn't help but laugh at her stance. Elizabeth's shoulders relaxed, and she giggled too.

'What's the plan then?'

I raised an eyebrow.

'You don't think I'm going to let you run off on your own, do you? Mia, we've been friends for a while now so you should understand this whole friendship bond by now.'

I smiled. She was right. The two of us had been through so much together, and we made a pretty good team.

'I'm looking for Sebastian,' I said, squaring my shoulders so she knew I wouldn't be swayed from my decision.

It worried me that someone I cared about might get hurt during my mission and I was about to express this when Ari piped up, 'They took that man to Hood Academy.'

'What man?' Elizabeth asked.

'The one in the white coat who was here earlier.' She pointed to a lab jacket hanging on a hook behind the door.

I knelt down, so I was eye level with the youngster. 'Are you sure?'

'Yes, I followed him and another man and saw them go through a back door with a red cross on it.'

'He's going to the lab,' Elizabeth said. 'That door leads to the nurse's station, and we both know where it goes from there.'

A shiver skittered down my spine at the memory of those clinical rooms, and the abysmal experiments that had taken place over God knows how many years.

'He could be visiting Felicity.' I dropped my head as I wondered for the millionth time about her injuries after our fight in the forest. Had she made a full recovery or was she seriously ill and in need of Sebastian's medical assistance?

'That girl would survive a nuclear blast.' Elizabeth squeezed my hand as if reading my mind. 'Whether he's there as a visitor, doctor, or psycho scientist, we at least know where to begin.'

She was right, of course, and it was thanks to Ari's super snooping skills.

'Well done, Ari.' I placed a hand on her shoulder as she beamed with pride. 'Now, I need you to go back to the farm.'

She pulled out of my grasp and crossed her arms over her tiny chest, that defiant glint returning to her eyes.

'I'm not going anywhere. We're a team. You need me.'

I had to admit that so far it was Ari who had found the barn, discovered Elizabeth's captor, and kept a beady eye on my movements. Maybe she would be useful – but from a safe distance. I couldn't risk her life.

'Okay, yes, we need you, but you will do *everything* me and Lizzie tell you, or I'm sending you home.'

Ari grinned and raised a small hand to her forehead. 'Aye, aye, Captain.'

Elizabeth covered her laugh with a hand and moved away to investigate the empty space. I could only gawp at the fierce little werewolf as she clicked her heels together and followed Lizzie. I prayed that keeping Ari close wasn't a mistake.

'Look at this.' Elizabeth handed me a scruffy notepad with a logo printed in the top corner. Evermore Pharmaceuticals. It was the same logo that had covered the boxes, which had recently occupied the small space where we stood.

'I've seen this before,' Ari said. 'This was the picture on the doctor's jacket. The man who injected my sister and me.'

Another link perhaps between the strange pharmaceutical company offering the cure to the packs and Sebastian. Did that mean the GA was in on it too?

Could an agency dedicated to upholding the hunters' oath really step over the line and be responsible for killing entire packs? Entire families? My blood ran cold thinking about it.

I pocketed the notepad and gave the room one last sweep with my torch. 'We're not going to find any answers here.'

Elizabeth smiled, but I could see the glimmer of fear shining in her eyes. We both knew what the next step entailed. We both understood that returning to Hood Academy was necessary, but neither of us needed another run-in with Felicity or the GA.

I squared my shoulders and faced my friends. 'It looks like we're going back to school.'

SIX

I knew my brother was going to be mad at me when he found out I'd gone, but part of me hoped that he knew me well enough to understand my reasons. Since finding my way back to him, I'd battled with those feelings of being an outsider. Not because I hadn't turned, although I knew that was an issue for Zak, but because I wasn't what everyone expected. They had listened to the tales of my violent life with Frank when Terry had spied on me at Zak's request, and then the stories I told them about Hood Academy. They listened, scowled, shook their heads in disgust, and welcomed me into the sanctuary of their home, but I think they were expecting me to be a weak, timid victim. I wasn't a victim. I refused to live my life in fear.

They hadn't been prepared for the survivor in me to be so strong and so I was left on the edges of their lives, circling like the runt of the litter trying to fight its way to the dinner bowl.

Maybe Zak thought he was getting his little sister back, the one who wore pigtails and pleats in her skirt. The little girl who had idolised her big brother before he abandoned her to a life of terror. Instead, he got a teenager with uncontrollable rage and trust issues.

Now wasn't the time to mope about not fitting in. As the daughter of a werewolf *and* a hunter, it was inevitable that I would be odd, but even I couldn't have guessed how peculiar my situation would be.

Elizabeth stopped suddenly in front of me, and I bumped into her, snapping out of my inner musings.

'What is it?' I hissed.

She pointed ahead, and I saw the flickering porch light above the nurse's office door. The windows to the main reception area were dark, and no sound came from the surrounding area.

'Just a short run across the car park and we're in.'

I manoeuvred my way in front of Elizabeth and assessed the area. The main school building loomed up on the right; no lights shone on the dormitory floors. In the distance, across the large expanse of lawn, I saw the patio doors leading to Adam's old room. The door had been blocked off with heavy timber strips following Elizabeth's rescue.

Ari tugged on my sleeve and nodded in the direction of the car park. Felicity and her father pushed their way through the nurse's office door and onto the gravel. As Mr Parker pressed something in his palm, a long black car lit up like a Christmas tree, the lights flashing in time to the loud beeps that bounced off the cold stone of the academy.

Felicity wore a tight bandage around her throat and nursed her arm in a sling. She hobbled as she followed her father to the car. Within minutes the engine roared to life, and they drove off down the winding driveway and out through the gates on to the main road into town.

The three of us let out a collective breath and then giggled.

'At least we know Parker and my arch-nemesis aren't home now.'

'That's a relief. I don't think I could cope with seeing you...' Elizabeth's words trickled to a stop, and she looked up at me with glassy eyes. 'I'm so sorry, Mia. I didn't want to bring up, you know, *that* fight.'

I understood her trepidation. Losing it completely and nearly killing someone wasn't a high point in my life and I didn't want to discuss it with her any more than she did with me.

'It's fine,' I said. 'Let's get on with finding Sebastian.'

We made sure the area was secure and sprinted across the gravel car park until we stood underneath the porch light. I reached up and unhooked the casing around the bulb, tapping it with my torch until it flickered out. Darkness was our friend.

Elizabeth tried the door; it was unlocked. I mulled this over as we entered the deserted reception area of the nurse's office. If the door was left unlocked, that meant Sebastian was free to leave at any point but chose to stay. Self-doubt bubbled in my gut as I wondered if Sebastian would be willing to help me or if his preference was to lock me up for his experiments.

Visions of my mum rushed forward: her smile, her perfume, her devotion to a man who I wasn't even aware was my father. She'd kept it a secret, even from Sebastian himself, choosing only to tell her best friend, Miss Ross. The experiments Sebastian had done on my mother were done with her blessing. She'd wanted a cure for lycanthropy, not just for herself, but for Zak and me too. She didn't want us to turn. She'd wanted a different kind of life for her children.

That decision cost her everything, but even until the bitter end she still believed Sebastian was doing something good. How then had his work become so twisted that he was injecting young girls like Ari and either killing them or forcing an early turn?

The school hospital wing was exactly as I remembered it. There was a reception area with a small office for the doctor, a storeroom, and four patient rooms. All the areas fed off a large circular space with direct access to the school through the office. To any unsuspecting visitor, it was a mundane hospital wing, but the seventh door, set into a dark alcove, led to another part of the school that only a select few knew existed. The laboratories.

For generations, these secret rooms had been used to experiment on werewolves. Sebastian's reason was to find a cure, but for the scientists who had come before him, the wolves were merely a tool and there to be violated, often killed in the process. Death clung to the walls.

I closed in on the seventh door, turning the handle slowly. Putting my shoulder against the metal, I pushed it open. As we had discovered during our time at Hood Academy, the laboratories were a row of single rooms each leading off one another. Like the rest of the nurse's area, the room we entered was in total darkness, but a sliver of light escaped from under the next door along.

Ari pointed at the floor, and I nodded to confirm I'd seen it. We had no way of knowing who or what lay beyond. It could be Sebastian, or it could be a room full of the Governors' Agency members.

'What do you want to do?' Elizabeth pressed close to ask the question, her fingers tightening around my arm as she spoke.

'There's only one thing we can do,' I said, and took a step towards the door.

Elizabeth sucked in a deep breath and grabbed Ari, wrapping an arm protectively around the child.

THE LIGHT WAS harsh against my eyes as I strode into the room. I didn't have any carefully laid-out plan about what to do next. I decided to adopt Miss Ross's fiery attitude and hope it paid off. As it turned out, the room was empty, and my attempt to look in control was wasted.

'It's okay, guys, you can come in.'

Elizabeth and Ari slid into the room behind me keeping to the edges as they took in the wall-to-ceiling shelving units filled with boxes upon boxes of pharmaceutical products. The logo we'd come across earlier was stamped on the side of every container.

The shelves took up all the wall space with smaller units dotted through the centre of the room. As far as I could tell, all the boxes were sealed and ready for shipping.

'Look at this!' Elizabeth motioned for me to join her.

She'd pulled one of the boxes out and was studying the label printed on the top.

'Its postal address is Cornwall. Miss Ross and Adam worked at the Cornish Academy before coming here.'

I took the small penknife I carried out of my pocket and slid the blade down the centre of the box. The label peeled apart as the box sprang open to reveal its contents.

Short silver tubes were bundled together in elastic bands. I pulled one free and lifted it up to the light. There was a tiny button on one end and when pushed a needle popped out from the opposite side.

Ari gasped and took a step back.

'That's what they gave my sister and me,' she said, a quiver in her voice.

I pushed the button and a green liquid ejected from the needle, spraying all over the floor. So this was Sebastian's serum. These tiny vials could kill, or destroy a child's life with the press of one button. I felt sick.

A loud crash from beyond the next door caused us all to yelp. The blood screamed in my ears as my heart thundered in my chest. Ari flew behind Elizabeth, and I once again doubted my decision to bring her along.

The door handle squealed as I turned it, giving away our position to whoever stood on the other side. It was too late to back out now, so I pushed on the door and let it swing wide.

THE COLOUR DRAINED from my face as I looked around the room. Elizabeth mumbled under her breath as she pushed Ari behind her.

There were five gurneys on either side of the room, ten beds in total, and each one contained a child, some no older than five or six. All wore brightly coloured pyjamas as if this was some upbeat children's ward. I fought against the rising nausea as I moved into the room. Behind the door, a silver tray lay upturned on the floor, its contents spilling out under the nearest bed. A young girl wriggled and squirmed, the terror in her eyes catching me off guard.

I held my hands up as I approached.

'We're not going to hurt you,' I said. 'We're here to help.'

I nodded at Elizabeth, and we both set to work checking each child for needle marks. Ari darted around the room connecting with each child and calming their distress. Seeing someone of their own age seemed to work and all ten captives gathered in the centre of the room looking up at me with an air of expectation.

'What are we going to do with them?'

Elizabeth's question vocalised the thoughts whirling through my head. What the hell were we going to do with them all? Had they been injected? Were they a danger to anyone, or themselves? Damn Sebastian for doing this.

The young girl who had knocked the tray over stepped forward like a pint-sized spokesperson.

'The doctor told us we would be cured if we behaved.' She spoke so quietly I had to lean forward to catch her words. 'He was lying, wasn't he?'

'What makes you say that?'

'They took us away from our families in the middle of the night. You don't do that if you want to cure someone.'

I couldn't argue with her logic, and I wondered if Sebastian had considered this approach.

'Who took you?'

She shrugged her shoulders. 'I don't know who they were; we'd never seen them before. The men wore black jumpers.'

'Men?' Elizabeth stepped forward. 'Not girls in grey jumpsuits?'

The girl shook her little blonde head.

Elizabeth turned her back to the group and leaned in to whisper, 'It wasn't Felicity or her goons then. Maybe Parker *is* using the GA to do his dirty work now.'

'We need to dig a bit deeper,' I said. 'There will be files in Sebastian's office. We need to get upstairs.'

We both looked over at the grubby faces of the children, their floaty hospital gowns making them look like a gaggle of ghosts at a Halloween party.

Before either of us could come up with an appropriate answer, Ari stepped forward and cleared her throat. 'Right you lot, it's time for us to leave. My friends need to stay and find the bad doctor, so you need to follow me.'

I was once again astounded at the resilience and strength of someone so young. I knelt down and pulled her into a tight hug.

'Thank you, Ari,' I whispered.

'Aye, aye, Captain.'

Elizabeth giggled and circled Ari into another embrace.

'Be careful, keep to the shadows, and follow the scent straight to the Mills farm. Zak will know what to do.'

The children followed Ari out of the door without question, their backs straight and senses tuned to their surroundings. I had no doubt in my mind that they would get home safely under Ari's supervision.

IT WAS JUST Elizabeth and me now. We knew there were no answers in the rooms we'd been through so the only route to take was forward.

'Let's go,' I said.

It didn't take us long to make it through to the room containing Hood Academy's secret filing cabinets. It was here I discovered the details about my mother's death, and that Sebastian was responsible for the death of Cody's family. It wasn't somewhere I ever thought I'd return to, but here we were digging through mounds of papers and drawers of notes.

I wished we knew what we were looking for. Evidence of Parker's diabolical scheme, Sebastian's involvement, the traitorous actions of the Governors' Agency, anything.

We were both so involved in our search that neither of us heard the door open until it was too late.

'What are you girls doing in here?'

I swung towards the voice, scattering papers across the floor as I went. Sebastian stood in the doorway, his face partly hidden in the shadows. He wore suit trousers and a pale blue shirt rolled up at the sleeves. Once upon a time his sheer presence would have filled the doorframe and radiated into any room filling it with his powerful energy. He didn't seem to be such an imposing figure as I once remembered. What had happened to break him? There was an ache in my chest as I took in the sight of the man standing before us, the man who studied me now with concern in his eyes.

'Mia, you came back.'

SEVEN

Sebastian stepped into the room and closed the door behind him cutting off the only route we had into the main school building, his expression leaving me in no doubt his action had been intentional.

I took a deep breath and squared my shoulders. What I needed to do went against everything I believed in, but this man, my father, was the only one who had the answers.

'I need your help, Sebastian.'

His face crumpled, and he let out a strangled cry. I couldn't prevent the pull I felt to offer him some support, but I also had a strong sensation to hit him and run away.

'I knew you'd come to me in the end,' he sobbed. 'Curing your lycanthropy was your mother's final wish, and I know she would be so happy that you've finally...'

I held my hand up to halt his ramblings.

'I'm not here for a cure, Sebastian, I'm here for answers.'

He recovered swiftly, wiping his eyes on the folds of his shirt-sleeves.

'I'm not sure I understand.'

'Your serum is being used across the country to kill children.'

He was shaking his head.

'No, no, that's not true. The serum was designed to *help* save the children from ever suffering the pain of turning. Evermore Pharmaceuticals thinks my work is groundbreaking and they've sent doctors out in the wolf community to share our work.'

'Is that why you had ten kids in there?' I jerked my thumb in the direction of the room we'd recently left. 'So you could *share* your work with them?'

Sebastian glanced between me and the door as he struggled with his conscience. I could see the conflict as it raged behind his eyes.

'You let them go.' It wasn't a question because he knew from my history that I would indeed have let them go. I gave a curt nod of my head.

'You shouldn't have done that, Mia. Mr Parker will be furious, and he will double his efforts to find and kill you.'

'What's Parker got to do with it?' I was fishing for information.

He shuffled his feet as he considered his answer.

'Mr Parker is a silent partner in Evermore Pharmaceuticals. It's his money that's funding our research and production.'

'It wasn't that long ago you called him a blackmailer.'

'I was wrong. Since becoming headmaster Mr Parker has opened up to my way of thinking. He told me he now believes in the work I'm doing for the good of the community.'

'Well, your silent partner is making you create a serum that kills most of the recipients or forces them to turn into werewolves earlier than they should. I've met a ten-year-old werewolf who watched her sister die after your filth was injected into them.'

'No, that's not possible, the serum is designed to prevent the werewolf gene from mutating. It acts as a blocker. I couldn't perfect a serum to reverse the transformation, which is why your mother died, but I'm still working on that. I hope to keep working on that to help you when you want it.'

'I will never want your help in that area, Sebastian. I'm happy the way I am and have no intention...'

'How can you be happy?' Sebastian interrupted me. 'You don't have the power to make a full shift. Your DNA is split between a hunter and a werewolf so you could never be a full-fledged wolf.'

I bristled at his words and sifted through my brain for possible solutions.

'Zak was born of a werewolf and a human, but he's an alpha!' I crossed my arms over my chest and stared defiantly at my father.

'Human DNA can be easily overridden by werewolf DNA, so any wolf who has a human mother or father will always have the wolf gene. You're different, Mia. You're a hybrid, and that's incredibly rare.'

I blinked.

'I'm a what?'

'A hybrid. You are a perfect fifty-fifty split of your mother and me. You're werewolf and hunter in equal parts. It's only after I saw you the other day that I realised. Hybrids are rare as not many hunters and werewolves mix, socially, let alone romantically. I found a few books on the topic if you want to read them.'

I saw Sebastian's gesture for what it was. He was offering me a truce by proposing to give me books that might answer my questions. Yes, his primary game plan was to strip me of my wolf side, but he understood my desire to find out more about who I was.

Elizabeth had remained silent throughout our exchange and only now approached to lay her hand on my arm.

'Mia, if Parker is behind this we need to stop him before he kills anyone else.'

I nodded and turned my attention back to Sebastian, as the look on his face shifted between anxiety and hope.

'If you can help us prove Mr Parker is using you and your serum to kill the packs' children then I'll...I'll take your DNA test so we can find out more.'

Elizabeth grabbed my hand. 'No, Mia. You can't trust him! He might inject you with God knows what and kill you like he did with your mum.'

I knew that I was risking so much by putting my trust and faith in a mad scientist, but he was also my father, my own flesh and blood. Staring into Sebastian's eyes, I saw something there that made me believe in him. Pride. His face shone with the kind of dewy glow that every parent gets when their child surpasses their expectations. It was something I could hold onto during the days and weeks to come. I was putting my faith in someone who had saved me then tried to destroy me in equal parts.

SEBASTIAN LED US up to the central school building and into the science classroom. Each wooden table had a Bunsen burner and microscope set up ready for the new term.

'Wait here.' Sebastian motioned for us to sit at one of the tables before hurrying out through a side door.

'I don't trust him,' Elizabeth hissed. 'What if he gets the GA?'

'We've got no choice, Lizzie.' I wriggled out of my coat and threw it on the nearest stool. 'He's the only one who can help us stop Parker, because he's here, on the inside.'

'He's not the only one on the inside.' A deep male voice carried across the room causing both of us to jump.

Adam stood in the doorway, a grin plastered across his handsome face. Elizabeth was off the chair and in his arms within seconds. I averted my eyes as they shared a moment. Reunited after so long.

'Good to see you again, Mia,' he said striding over to where I was sitting.

I embraced my friend, clinging to him for longer than was probably acceptable. Having him here filled me with joy, not only for my best friend but also for our cause. Adam had always been a tower of strength during our past adventures.

'What are you doing here? Not that I'm not thrilled to see you.'

Adam chuckled. 'Miss Ross called and told me about Lizzie being taken in for questioning. By the time I'd driven up from Cornwall she was free.' He folded Elizabeth into a warm embrace and kissed the tip of her nose. 'Sebastian told me you were here.'

A lightness filled my chest at Adam's words. It was good to have him back, and good that Sebastian hadn't reacted negatively to him being here.

'Does Zak know we're here?' I dreaded the reply, but Adam laughed and slapped a big brown hand on my shoulder.

'Let's say, I wouldn't want to be you when you get home.'

Shit!

'Right.' Sebastian returned with a large cardboard box. He placed it on the counter and shifted it so the pharmaceutical logo faced the other way. 'I'm going to show you, scientifically, what the serum can do.'

He opened the box and took out one of the silver tubes, unscrewing the cap. He flipped the switch on the monitor linked to his microscope and placed a glass slide on the counter where he emptied some of the liquid out.

'Hmm, that's odd,' he mumbled.

'What is?'

'Well, it shouldn't be green.'

He lifted the slide and carefully slid it under the clips to hold the plate in place, fiddling with the focus controls on the side of the equipment. Leaning over the microscope, he studied the liquid through the eyepiece.

Green swirls filled the monitor screen, and we waited for his scientific explanation. He fiddled with the controls. We waited some more.

'Well? Are you going to give us this science lesson or not?' I asked.

Sebastian stood up and moved away from the microscope, running his hands through his hair in that agitated manner that always worried me.

'This isn't my serum,' he said. 'It's been modified.'

We all watched the screen. It could have been a photograph of the Aurora Borealis for all we knew. The patterns smeared across the image bled from deep green to yellow.

'What do you mean by *modified*?'

He snapped into action, opening the desk drawer and rummaging around until he found a small glass vial. Inching the glass plate out of its restraints he replaced it with a fresh slide and emptied the new, clear liquid out.

The monitor changed the image to show us what looked like a clear puddle with tiny grey blobs floating through the middle of it.

'That,' he stabbed a finger at the screen, 'is what my serum looks like. The serum that prevents a child from turning. I don't know what *this* is.' He waved a hand at the green blob oozing off the rejected slide. It was like toxic waste compared to the clean image on the screen.

Opening up the box, Sebastian tipped out more of the silver tubes and began unscrewing the caps. All the contents were green.

'Can you work out what modifications were made?' Adam asked.

'Not from here. I need my equipment.'

'Let's take it downstairs to the lab then,' I said, already halfway to the door.

'No, my lab isn't here at school, it's at my home.'

'But, I thought you lived here, at the school.'

Clearly it hadn't been on his to-do list to share with his only relative the simple fact that he lived off-site. I felt the strangest feeling of rejection but pushed it aside.

'No, I have a house in the forest, near the edge of town. It's been in my family for generations, but I've never disclosed the whereabouts. Not even the GA or Parker know where it is.'

In that single moment, I realised Sebastian wasn't all bad. For him to own up to the existence of a safe house made me feel warm inside.

'Let's pack up and go then. The faster we get you to your equipment, the faster we can work out what Parker has done and stop him.'

Sebastian scanned the room as if seeing us all for the first time.

'We don't have time. If what you say is true and this modified serum can kill then we need to stop the distribution. It will take me much too long to work out what they've done and rectify it.'

'Okay, so you think stopping the distribution is the best plan, but how do we do that? I wouldn't know where to start.' I realised there was a hint of panic in my voice. We weren't dealing with overdue homework here, this was serious, up to your neck in danger stuff, and as I looked around the room, I noticed everyone was looking at me.

Elizabeth moved first, rushing towards me but deviating at the last second to spin the box at my side. The Evermore Pharmaceuticals logo glared up at us. Of course! We knew who the distributor was; now all we had to do was shut them down.

SEBASTIAN'S OFFICE HAD almost changed beyond all recognition. His desk was still the same and dominated the centre of the room, but the books were absent, the paintings stripped from the walls, and the photo frames containing the happy images of my mum gone, to be replaced by the smarmy grin of my nemesis, Felicity, and other people I didn't recognise. Parker had commandeered the headmaster's office after the incident with Sebastian and me on the back lawn.

I wasn't surprised that Sebastian had been sacked. It was either that or a suspension at the very least. Instead, it appeared that Mr Parker had taken full control of the academy and relegated Sebastian to the laboratories below the school, a bit like Frankenstein locked away in his lair.

I shook the thoughts from my mind and walked across to the mahogany desk, tugging at the desk drawers in search of clues. The smaller drawers opened without any issue, and an assortment of pens, pencils, and elastic bands spilled out when I tipped them onto the floor. The slim-fronted middle drawer, however, remained locked. I flipped open my penknife and set to work, hacking at the lock until I heard the crunch and click.

It slid open revealing two folders sitting side by side. The blue file on the right contained a list of the hunter academies around the UK and the last known whereabouts of the country's packs. I stuffed it into my backpack, hoping the information might come in handy in the future. The folder on the left was thicker and included pages of formulas, photographs of indigenous tribes, information on plants and herbs and, most importantly, an address for the Evermore Pharmaceuticals warehouses in Nottingham.

'Jackpot!'

BY THE TIME I returned to the nurse's office my friends and Sebastian were waiting. Adam had packed bags full of supplies and was off-loading one of them on Elizabeth who giggled as the weight nearly tipped her over. Sebastian was wearing a short navy coat and walking boots with a large holdall strapped across his chest. His brow creased as I walked in clutching the thick folder.

'Thought this might be helpful,' I said handing it over to him. He flipped open the cover and thumbed through the images.

'Interesting. It seems Mr Parker's frequent visits to the native tribes might have something to do with the modification of the serum. It's possible that he used a herb or plant root.'

'The science of how and why is your department, Sebastian, I'm only interested in the address for Evermore.'

'You found it!'

I nodded. 'There's a warehouse in Nottingham. That's the closest one, so I think we should start there. At least it means we can keep the local packs safe while we deal with the rest of the distribution centres.'

I looked at the expectant faces of my friends and smiled.

'Are you sure you're up for this?'

Adam laughed, and it bubbled up from deep in his throat.

'You really think we're going to let you do this without us, Mia? No way, we're in this together. We're family.'

My heart threatened to split wide open at his words. Family. My real family was fractured beyond belief. Mum was dead, my brother had murdered my stepdad, and my biological dad was, well, he was trying. Elizabeth and Adam, on the other hand, believed that family extended beyond your DNA, and they made all the horror and danger we faced worth fighting for.

EIGHT

We drove in silence, Adam taking control of Sebastian's black SUV. Elizabeth sat up front with her boyfriend, not wanting to let him out of her sight after so long apart, and I rode in the back with Sebastian. He had been poring over the contents of the folder for a while, his jaw set in a hard line as he delved further into the information.

'Find anything useful?' I asked.

'Hmm?' He lifted his head slowly as if only just realising he wasn't on his own. 'Oh, yes, it would be quite brilliant if it wasn't so awful. Mr Parker appears to have travelled extensively to search for a specific species of plant. His notes refer to the strychnine tree found in Southeast Asia.'

'Strychnine? As in rat poison?'

'Yes, exactly. I'm impressed you knew that, Mia.'

I huffed. 'I might not have participated a whole lot in science class, but I did listen.'

'Well, the tree contains the poison, and for many years it was used as a common rodenticide, but somehow he has genetically engineered it to blend with my serum. Strychnine causes deadly muscular convulsions, the type of convulsions you would experience during a turn on the full moon.'

'So it's hidden in plain sight because the packs would expect their children to be convulsing?'

'Precisely! What's interesting is that some of the children are able to fight it. Did you say you'd met one who had turned early?'

'Ari, she's ten years old and a fledgling wolf.' I smiled as I thought about her. She was going to make an impressive wolf one day. 'She was taken with her sister up in Yorkshire to receive your so-called cure. Her sister didn't make it.'

'Interesting.' Sebastian's head bobbed up and down as he took in this information and flicked back through the notes.

'Why did Ari survive but her sister didn't?' I asked, hoping I could give Ari and her family some useful information to ease their grief.

'I'm not sure, it's actually more fascinating that your friend survived at all as this stuff should, by rights, kill anyone who takes it!'

'So Parker is distributing a flawed serum under the secret protection of a pharmaceutical company who claim to be sympathetic to the werewolf cause. They're enticing the pack leaders to hand over their children with the hope of a cure.'

'It certainly seems that way.'

'Why would they want to do that? Surely if the alphas cured their kids, the werewolf lines would come to an end.'

Sebastian put down the folder and glanced over at me, his eyes showing a warmth I had never seen before. Or perhaps never noticed.

'Your mother wanted you and Zak to receive a cure so you wouldn't have to go through the pain of turning or having the burning desire to hunt and kill.'

I was briefly reminded of my run-in with Felicity and the fact I'd nearly killed her in my heightened emotional state.

'Not all wolves hunt and kill,' I said, thinking of all the packs I'd met so far.

'Sometimes you don't have a choice, the turn changes you mentally as well as physically, and any harm you inflict is often done without intention.'

Again I thought about Felicity. Had I intended to finish her off? Was I capable of killing her, or of killing anyone? It was true that the wolf side of my personality was ruled by emotions, and I had been struggling to control this, but could it drive me to take a human life?

Sebastian continued. 'As a parent, you would want to do everything in your power to keep your child safe. Just because the alphas are giving their pack the option to prevent a turn doesn't mean they forfeit the lifestyle and community of the pack.'

'I guess so. Although...' I looked away and watched the shadows whip past the car window as I tried to sort out my jumbled thoughts. 'I don't think I belong in a pack, being a hybrid like you said. I feel like I've got one foot in the hunter camp and the other in the pack, but I don't really belong to either.'

Sebastian leaned over and placed his hand over mine.

'Sometimes you create your own pack without even realising it.'

He patted my hand and inclined his head towards Elizabeth and Adam. My pack. I'd been so hung up about being an outsider that I hadn't noticed what I was creating within my circle of friends. We all watched over each other, cared for one another, like a proper pack would. I felt a tug in my chest as I realised, almost for the first time, that I did belong somewhere after all.

Sebastian rummaged around in his bag and pulled out a notebook. It had a creamy golden cover and well-worn pages. He handed it to me with a small smile.

I flicked it open and the word *hybrid* jumped out at me.

'It might help answer a few of your questions,' he said.

I flipped open the first page and began reading, absorbed in the notes scribbled in the book.

The power of the pack runs through their veins, and yet the strength, discipline, and leadership qualities of the hunter are also clearly prominent

It went on to talk about the dual personality of a hybrid, and I was about to laugh at the similarities between me and the notes when Adam broke into my thoughts as he slowed the car down and switched off the headlights.

'We're here!'

We all gazed up at the imposing structure looming out of the darkness. The warehouse was long and thin, its plain grey walls stretching for at least a mile behind to a newly constructed glass entrance, the Evermore logo emblazoned across the top half of the glass with a smoky background to help it stand out.

'Okay, so what do we do now?' Elizabeth's bright blue eyes were wide as she turned in her seat to look back at me.

'We burn it down.' It was the only way I could think of destroying all the serum and prevent the facility from being used. Yes, we could break in and steal the boxes, but that would only put a dent in their sickening plans; I wanted to obliterate them.

THERE WAS A large docking area near the back of the warehouse where two trucks were parked up presumably awaiting their shipments. Adam broke into one and confirmed it was empty, but the other had already been loaded.

'Perhaps we could steal this one,' suggested Sebastian as he climbed into the truck's cab. 'I'm sure I could drive it if necessary.'

'Maybe later, we need to destroy the warehouse first. Did you see any security?'

Adam nodded. 'There are two guards at the front of the building. One of them is asleep at the desk and the other is watching a late-night chat show. If we're careful, we can be in and out before they know it.'

'Okay, let's get on with it.'

We all squeezed under the roller shutter door that Adam and Sebastian had managed to pry open with a crowbar from the truck. From the outside it shouldn't be immediately obvious that anything was amiss if the security guards were to venture out of the comfort and warmth of their office and do a patrol.

The inside space was cavernous, with high ceilings, and long racking units stretching the full length of the storeroom. Thousands of boxes displayed the Evermore logo.

'How do we know which boxes contain the serum?'

It hadn't occurred to me that Evermore probably supplied other products as well as Parker's evil werewolf-killing serum. Did we have time to sort through them all?

'We're going to have to burn it all.' It was the only option. Time wasn't on our side. Parker would sweep across the country like a disease making sure every pack was offered the *cure;* he wouldn't hesitate in his actions, and I had to adopt the same attitude.

We searched around the store until we found five large containers of cleaning fluid with a Warning: Highly Flammable sign on the packaging and began to soak the boxes, leaving a trail in the hope that one box would ignite the next and so on. Once done we all stood by the exit and took in a collective breath. This was it.

Adam lit the match and threw it into the nearest box. It caught light at once and began to crackle and pop as the flames devoured the cardboard.

'We need to leave, now! Once the fire reaches the silver tubes filled with the serum, they'll go up like fireworks, and goodness knows what else this place is storing.'

We scurried under the door and rolled out onto the packing area, taking in a great lungful of air to rid ourselves of the cloying scent of cleaning fluid. The flames reached the first tube as we jumped down onto the tarmac, and the bang caused us all to drop to our knees instinctively. One after the other the boxes exploded, and smoke poured out from under the shutter door.

We pushed backward, breaking into a sprint as the booms got louder, rushing for Sebastian's SUV and the protection it offered.

The entire warehouse was ablaze now, and none of us could turn our faces away as the fire tore through the structure. The speed at which it moved both startled and impressed me.

The glass entrance shattered under the intense heat, spraying shards of the blackened Evermore logo over the car park. The two bewildered security guards stumbled out of the main door sprinting for safety, and as we drove away, the back wall buckled and fell, crushing the two trucks in the loading area under the twisted metal struts.

None of us spoke. Adam sped away and only switched on the headlights when we were at a safe distance. We passed a police car and three fire engines tearing down the main road towards the warehouse oblivious to the fact that they'd been so close to the arsonists responsible for the destruction they were about to find.

'Well, that's one down,' said Adam breaking the tension in the car. 'Where do we go next?'

Sebastian shuffled the files in his lap and opened up the folder containing the academies and locations of the packs.

'Looking at the schedule in Parker's files it says a shipment was delivered to Somerset yesterday, which means they should be rolling out the injections in the next few hours.'

I squinted at the clock on the dashboard, 4 a.m. If we pushed hard, we might make it in time to stop any of the children receiving the serum.

Adam caught my eye in the mirror and winked. 'Somerset then?' he asked.

'Somerset it is,' I confirmed.

MY HEAD BOUNCED off the car window as I was jolted awake. Sebastian snored softly from his seat next to me, and Elizabeth's head hung forward cradled by her seat belt. The sun had risen and as I rubbed my eyes and stretched, I glanced around at the scenery flashing by.

'Welcome to sunny Somerset,' Adam said from the driving seat.

'I'm so sorry, Adam. I never meant to fall asleep and leave all the driving up to you.'

'Do you drive?'

'Well, no, obviously, but Sebastian could have taken over for a while.' I looked across at my father as his mouth hung open and a little snore escaped. 'Or maybe not!'

We both giggled, and I wriggled forward in my seat so I could chat with my friend.

'Do you think we'll find the alpha in time?'

I shook my head. 'I'm not sure. I hope we can, but these Evermore doctors have been so convincing in their argument that no alpha, or parent for that matter, could resist putting their child forward for a lycanthropy cure.'

'Would you take it if you could?'

It was a valid question and one I'd contemplated several times when Sebastian locked me in the hospital wing all those months ago.

'I don't know. It's not like I'm a full werewolf. I don't have to experience the excruciating pain of every bone in my body breaking and re-setting. For me, it was easy, apart from my gum aching where the fangs slide out.'

'What's it like? Did anything else change for you?'

'Everything changed. I can hear what people are saying when they're far away, and all the smells are stronger too. It's pretty neat apart from this thirst to rip people's throats out.'

Adam laughed. 'By *people* you mean Felicity.'

'Uh-huh, I only stopped because Zak turned up and did his alpha mojo on me. Don't get me wrong, I'm glad he stopped me, but up until that moment I would have happily sliced her throat open.'

'Good to know, I'll be sure to stay on your good side then.'

I punched him on the arm and laughed.

Elizabeth stirred in her seat and gave a little sigh. 'Is it morning already?'

Adam slipped his hand into hers. 'Only just.'

Sebastian yawned from behind me, and I sat back to take in the sight of my friends and family, fighting by my side to right a terrible wrong done to the werewolf community. It felt good to be doing something worthwhile.

THE PACK LIVED in the woods near the Somerset Hunters Academy, and as we approached the turn for the alpha's house, we saw the school from the road. It was nothing like Hood Academy. Instead of the grandiose setting of Hood's majestic gardens and historical backdrop, this school occupied a modern building with tinted glass windows, and resembled an office block rather than an establishment for werewolf hunters.

'Ugh, it's ugly!' Elizabeth agreed with my first impression.

'The GA have spent large sums renovating this centre following a recent fire.' Sebastian said. 'They wanted it to be the flagship school for the UK.'

I huffed. 'Well it needs burning down again.'

'Oh no! We're not going to burn this place to the ground too, are we?'

I laughed at the squeal in Elizabeth's voice and the unintentional way she still scrubbed at her hands where it appeared the cleaning fluid had irritated her skin.

'No, Lizzie. We'll leave this one standing. We're here to prevent the wolves from getting that serum and nothing else. If we can do what we need to without the hunters even knowing we were here then that's even better.'

Adam pulled off the main road opposite the academy and drove for a mile down a dirt track, which ended at a scenic wooded picnic area. As we all climbed out of the car to stretch our legs, I heard the roar of the sea in the distance.

I turned my face up to catch the early morning sun. There was no real warmth in it yet, but it held the promise of a pleasant day ahead, which was a blessing as I realised I'd left my coat behind at Hood Academy. I tuned my senses in to listen to the surrounding wildlife noises and picked up something different, a commotion that wasn't at home in this environment. It almost sounded like a playground chant, or a bully taunting their victim. Before I could mention anything to my friends, a shrill scream tore through the wind.

I broke into a run, sprinting towards the sound, my senses switching on to full alert. I could hear Lizzie and Adam running after me, crashing through the trees in pursuit. There was a dull ache in my jaw, and I realised my fangs had slid forward, and the pounding in my head increased with every slap of my feet against the dry path.

A second scream ricocheted off the trees, and I adjusted my route, breaking through the treeline and heading deeper into the woods. Nothing could have prepared me for what I found.

Three young children, no more than twelve years old, thrashed around on the ground, their bodies twisting and convulsing as the pain shot through their tiny frames. One black-haired boy and three girls stood over them all dressed in the grey jumpsuits I recognised as the hunters' uniform. Instead of helping the children, they watched the spectacle like it was paid entertainment.

Bursting into the small clearing, I growled at the hunters, startling them into action. By the surprised looks on their faces they'd never seen a hybrid, or at the very least they'd never seen a wolf in the daylight. Their wooden staffs lifted in unison as they circled towards me. From the nervous glances they gave each other, they were unsure how to deal with me. One last look at the children pushed any rational thoughts I had aside and angered me enough to snarl at the foursome. My claws flicked out as I shook my hands and flexed them, clicking the nails together. Beads of sweat covered each of the students' foreheads and the sound of their hearts pounding filled me with surprising joy. I wanted them to fear me, I wanted them to panic and forget their training, and part of me wanted them to run so I could hunt each of them down.

Adam burst through the trees causing one of the hunters to cry out.

'Help us!' she yelled, her eyes imploring my friend to assist them.

Adam ignored her pleas and moved towards the children, kneeling beside them to check their pulse and try to calm the convulsions. Lizzie arrived soon after and skirted around the edge of the clearing to Adam's side. After checking on the children and her boyfriend, she moved to stand next to me.

'Who are you?' It was the boy who spoke, taking a step forward in a bid to assert his authority. I growled, and he jumped back.

Elizabeth ignored him. 'You're students at the academy.' It wasn't a question. 'How many children have been injected with that serum?'

'How do you know about the serum?'

'Because I'm the one who created it.' Sebastian walked into the clearing and stalked over to where the children writhed on the floor in agony. He flipped open a bag and took out a small flask. 'Here, get them to drink this, it might help with the pain.' He handed Adam the container and leaned in closer as my friend whispered something in Sebastian's ear. He nodded and squared his shoulders before moving to my side.

'I'm Dr Roberts from Hood Academy in Nottingham, and the serum you are using on these innocents is defective. I'm here to recall all vials.'

His voice boomed with authority, and I shifted my stance so I could study him. He looked like he did the night he first walked into my life: dignified, strong, and someone to be respected. Adam had no doubt instructed Sebastian on what to say but he had played his part well. A bubbling of pride lit up my chest.

'We weren't told about any recall. Headmaster Gregory sent us out to do a job, and we've done it.' The boy gestured towards the children. 'Killing werewolves is what the hunters' oath is all about after all.' He slid his predatory gaze upon me, and I felt the corners of my mouth curl into a snarl.

'Bring it on,' I whispered flexing my claws once more.

Elizabeth stepped in front of me sensing my need to lunge forward and tear the kid's face off.

'Our friend is a hybrid, she is part wolf, and part hunter so she understands our oath perfectly well. We don't want to fight you; we just want to stop the killing of innocent children.'

'Well, sweetheart, that's too bad because we came out here for a fight and so that's what you're gonna get.'

For a moment I wondered if we'd found the male version of Felicity before snapping into action and leaping forward to knock the closest girl to the ground. She screamed and dropped her staff, which rolled harmlessly away. Her eyes sparked with fear as I traced a claw down the side of her face.

'Leave this place before I rip you apart piece by piece.' I growled.

She was on her feet and running before her friends could help. Another girl joined her and disappeared into the treeline.

The boy rounded his staff on me and stood his ground. If I wasn't so overcome with rage, I might have been impressed. Lizzie approached the remaining girl, her fists held high as she prepared to fight alongside me.

'Come on then, sweetheart; let's see what a hybrid's made of.'

I heard Sebastian's audible tut as he stepped aside to give me room to manoeuvre. I didn't need the extra space, I only needed enough room to reach across and cut the idiot's cheek. He cried out, and it felt good.

'Nobody calls me sweetheart apart from my boyfriend.' He'd picked the wrong person if it was a fight he was after. Felicity nearly lost her life for calling me wolf girl, so this smarmy kid was in serious trouble. I knew I needed to rein it in this time, as Zak wasn't around to use his alpha connection.

The boy's staff flew through the air and connected with my shoulder. I flinched but shook off the pain, swinging my arm out to smash the wood from his grasp. It hit the floor, breaking into two pieces. The hunter wasn't finished though and pushed forward punching me first in the face and then in the stomach. My cheek stung from the blow, and the ache in my jaw intensified, but I didn't go down. He advanced again, but I swung my leg out high in a roundhouse kick connecting with the side of his head. He dropped like a stone, blood pouring from his ear.

'Enough!' I screamed, the sound echoing off the surrounding trees.

Lizzie held on to the girl's arms as she squirmed and tried to flee, clearly eager to leave the boy to fend for himself.

'I don't think much of your hunter friends,' I said standing over him. 'Two have deserted you and she looks seconds away from ditching your ass. So much for looking after each other and uniting against the common enemy.'

He spat at my feet. '*They* are the common enemy.' He pointed at the children.

'No,' I said. 'They're kids who happen to have been born to werewolf families; they didn't ask for this.'

I realised my voice sounded normal again and a quick check of my hands proved my claws had retracted and the fangs had disappeared. I was Mia again.

'What's your name?'

The boy looked up at me, his green eyes filled with loathing. 'Ethan,' he replied.

I held out my hand to help him up and his brow creased as he contemplated slapping it away or accepting it. 'I'm Mia, and this is Lizzie, Adam, and Sebastian.'

He wrinkled his nose as he took my hand, acting as if I might infect him with some deadly disease. I pulled him to standing where he began dusting off his jumpsuit. I was half expecting him to run, but he didn't.

'I won't say it's a pleasure to meet you,' he mumbled.

'We're not the enemy, Ethan. We're trying to help save these children. Evermore Pharmaceuticals have misled the packs by offering to administer a cure for lycanthropy that doesn't exist. There's a Mr Parker at our academy who's determined to wipe out the werewolf gene for good by killing the innocent.'

'Well, this Mr Parker of yours has probably succeeded,' he said. 'These three were the last of the Somerset packs to receive the serum. We were tasked with escorting them back to their parents after the injections.'

'Instead, you brought them here, and you would have happily watched them die.' Elizabeth was angry, and her eyes flared with unspoken words. She'd released her grip on Ethan's companion, who now took a step back before speaking up.

'We were told that some of the kids might react badly to the injection and if that was the case we should—'

'Kill them!' Elizabeth finished the sentence for her, disgust written all over her face.

'Yes,' the girl mumbled. 'But *he* forced us to do it. Told us he'd get us kicked out if we disobeyed.'

'Who did?'

Ethan crossed his arms over his chest and sneered.

'She's talking about me.'

'What gives you the right to condemn these kids?' I could feel my pulse quickening as I eyed the arrogant boy in front of me.

'Our job is a pretty easy one, sweetheart. We destroy the wolves who threaten our town. Simple as that.'

I bristled at his words. It appeared he'd chosen to disregard my earlier threat about calling me sweetheart. I'd never wanted to slap someone so much in my life.

'No, it's not that simple. These children never asked to be wolves, their parents never asked for it either. They are what they are, and we are what we are.'

Ethan laughed. 'I don't think anyone knows what *you* are.'

I ignored his attempts to goad me and turned my attention to the girl.

'I doubt your headmaster knows the truth about what's going on here,' I said. She was shrivelling up on herself under Ethan's glare. She shook her head.

'I suggest you go back and tell him what's happened. Make sure he knows that the serum is flawed.'

The girl nodded and sprinted off in the direction of the academy.

Sebastian cleared his throat. 'It's obvious that we arrived too late, but hopefully, we can get these youngsters back to their families and help save their lives.'

'Agreed. Ethan will lead us to the packs.'

'What? No, are you crazy? I'm not going to any wolf den and I'm certainly not helping *you*.'

I stood millimetres from his face and growled at him.

'You are going to help me and my friends, and you are going to help save these kids, or we'll let your headmaster know how you twisted his orders for your own sick benefit. I'm fairly sure you'll be expelled and I dread to think what happens to rogue hunters. It's not up for debate.'

His shoulders slumped and I watched his Adam's apple bob up and down in time to his heartbeat.

'Hand over your weapons and phone.'

The muscle in his jaw flinched as he turned out his pockets. Adam confiscated his knives and I pocketed his mobile.

'You'll get them back when you've earned it,' I said.

Turning away from the reckless hunter, I spoke to my friends. 'Once the kids are returned we need to get a message to Zak, so he knows what's going on. The packs need to know the danger they're in and unite before Evermore wipes everyone out.'

NINE

I t felt a little bit like going home as we arrived at the tiny house on the beach. Although the building was painted white and looked nothing like the Mills farm, it had a similar vibe to it. A warmth seeped out of every crack in the plaster and the curls of paint at the window frames. A low fence ran around the property bordering a small patch of land with a bench seat facing the sea. I longed to sit and stare at the ocean but the three children we'd rescued needed help.

'The infusion I gave them should help with the convulsions and hopefully counteract the effects of the poison.' Sebastian filled in the anxious parents as they crowded around the children in a spare bedroom. I watched from the doorway and felt a sense of pride as he handled them with care and consideration.

He hadn't even managed that with me on our first meeting, in fact, he'd been so cold and calculating that I half suspected he regretted having a hormonal teenager dumped into his life. I watched as he scooped up the young girl and fluffed the pillow beneath her head, settling her more comfortably. He checked their pulse points, replenished the moist flannels on their foreheads, and cautiously engaged with their werewolf parents on the health of their offspring.

'Can't believe it's the same man from a few months ago, can you?' Adam folded his arms across his chest and leaned against the doorframe. His dark skin still glistened from the exertion of carrying the children through the forest to safety.

'Mmm, he's made a remarkable turnaround.'

Adam raised an eyebrow as he glanced across at me and I rolled away from the doorframe and walked further along the corridor to a small window overlooking the beach.

'You don't sound convinced,' he said catching up to me. I knew there'd been a hint of scepticism in my tone and I also knew Adam would pick up on that as I was fairly certain both he and Elizabeth felt the same.

'I don't know what to think,' I said. 'Sebastian locked me in a hospital room with the intention of experimenting on me! He even shot Terry! Yes, he's helped us, and yes, he seems to be committed to stopping Evermore, but am I supposed to accept that he's a good guy now?'

'What's your gut telling you?'

'My gut?'

'Yeah, you've always been powered by your intuition, Mia. You've got determination and strength, but you're also smart. Both Lizzie and I trust that you'll always do the right thing because, well, that's how you roll.'

I smiled up at my friend. It was nice to receive such a compliment. I'd tried so hard to fit in with the academy students and then with the pack, but that feeling of being an outsider hadn't gone away, so to be complimented on my qualities felt good.

'Honestly, I *want* to believe that he's changed. I want Sebastian to step up and help us defeat Parker and Felicity, Evermore, and the GA. I want him to understand why this is so important to me.'

'And you want him to be the dad you never had.'

Adam's words stopped me short. He was right. Sebastian was my biological father, and I longed to have that father-daughter relationship.

'Yes, I want him to be everything and more. It's not too much to ask, is it?'

We laughed, and Adam threw his muscular arm around my shoulder and squeezed.

'I'm sure he'll manage it, and if not, we can always set the werewolves on him.'

WE WERE STILL giggling as we joined Lizzie in the garden.

'What are you two plotting?' She was sitting on the garden bench with her long legs stretched out in front of her.

'Sebastian's downfall if he doesn't behave himself.' Adam dropped onto the seat next to her and nuzzled her neck.

'Sounds fair to me.' She giggled.

I was about to lay out the terms and conditions of Sebastian's sentence should he mess it all up when a large man wearing biker leathers and a bright red bandana sprinted up the path towards us.

'Where's Liam? Where's the alpha?'

A sheen of sweat covered his face, and from the deep creases on his brow, he wasn't here to deliver good news.

Like a game of Chinese whispers, the Somerset pack members passed the stranger's arrival along the line until the alpha, Liam, a tall man with a quiet temperament, emerged from the front door. The biker wolf rushed to his side pulling him into a private huddle.

I watched amused as the large man flung his arms in all directions, reliving the scene from whatever had him so spooked. I hoped that the academy hadn't retaliated after our intercepting them in the woods earlier and looked around to see if Ethan was still with us. The black-haired hunter sat with his back to the cottage wall also watching the events unfold.

I wandered over and sat next to him ignoring the stiffness in his posture at my arrival.

'I'm not the enemy, Ethan. You do know that, don't you?'

'If you're not a hunter then you're my enemy, sweetheart.'

'So that's it then.' I threw my arms in the air. 'There's no fine line, and no benefit of the doubt? You're either a good guy or a bad guy?'

He chuckled and pulled at a long blade of grass. 'We're not living in some superhero movie, Mia. The hunters and wolves don't mix, it's been that way for hundreds of years. If you followed the hunters' oath then you'd understand that.'

'Is that what's bothering you, that I broke my oath?'

'Doesn't it bother you?' He leaned forward and turned his body so he was facing me, his green eyes sparkling under the bright sunshine. 'You trained alongside hunters, you lived and socialised with them, and you upheld the rules of the oath, but you lied to them. You turned your back on everyone and joined the wolves.'

I was stunned by the passion in his voice. There was no doubt that he was a loyal hunter but I knew it wasn't that black and white. Especially not at Hood Academy.

'There was no malice involved in me leaving, Ethan. My friends understood why I had to follow the pack and they supported me.'

'I could never support any friend who turned their back on the oath.'

Ethan leaned back against the house and resumed watching Liam and the biker's exchange. He obviously didn't have anything else to say to me on the matter.

'How the hell you have any friends at all is a mystery to me,' I mumbled, standing up and dusting off my jeans.

I REJOINED ELIZABETH and Adam. I didn't want them to, but Ethan's words had hit a nerve. I was about to talk to Lizzie about it when I caught sight of Liam and the biker man staring at me. The compassion in their eyes turned my blood to ice, and I slowly slid onto the bench.

'What's up?' Elizabeth nudged me and then followed my line of sight. 'Oh.'

Liam approached, and I fought against the nausea that threatened to take over me. Whatever news the biker had delivered was either about me or for me, of that I was certain.

'Mia, can I have a word?' The gentle lulling of Liam's voice put me at ease as I stood and followed him to the garden gate.

'There's been an incident at Hood Academy,' he said.

Relief washed over me. An incident at the academy wasn't my primary concern, but as an ex-student and Sebastian's daughter I guessed Liam felt obliged to tell me.

'It appears that a rescue attempt was made, but the pack were low in numbers and were overwhelmed by the GA in residence.'

I nodded my head as I processed this information. Why was he telling me this? Who had needed rescuing?

'The alpha and his team swept through the grounds, but when they engaged with the GA, they suffered a great number of casualties. Many of the pack were injured but managed to escape, but a few were captured.'

I listened to the words, and I watched the movement of Liam's lips as he passed on the animated message from the biker wolf, but something failed to connect in my brain. Seemingly understanding my predicament, Liam filled in the blanks for me.

'They have your alpha and his second, Byron, plus two others. We have no more information at the moment.'

'No! They can't. Zak's my brother. They're my friends. Why would they go to the school? I don't understand. Cody! What about Cody?' I could hear the desperation in my voice.

'I'm sorry, Mia, I don't know anything more than what I've told you, but I want you to know that you have the full support of my pack. If you want our help you only have to ask.'

I COULDN'T DIFFERENTIATE between the roar in my head and the roar of the waves as they crashed against the rocks. Both sounds were angry and loud. I'd allowed Adam to take over the conversation with Liam as my distress erupted into full-blown hysteria. Lizzie led me away clinging to my hand like a frightened child, the pair of us trying to comprehend what had happened since our departure.

For the next hour or so I'd screamed, cried, and ranted at Sebastian as if he was responsible for my brother's capture. It hadn't helped when my dear old dad began explaining the probable procedure Parker would use on my brother to Liam's assembled pack members.

I'd stormed out slamming the door so hard I'm sure I heard glass break somewhere.

The sea air didn't have the calming effect I'd hoped for, so I set off at a brisk pace across the sand towards the small lighthouse. Why had Zak advanced on Hood Academy? The only people who needed rescuing when we were there had returned home already. The biker wolf confirmed that Ari had made it back with the other children and they were all accounted for. We'd left nobody behind.

I shivered against the cool breeze that hinted at the end of summer and kicked myself once again for leaving my coat behind. My coat. My scent. A slow-motion film began to play out in my mind. The images were of me climbing down the trellis from my bedroom window and dashing through the woods, arriving at the barn in search of clues as to Sebastian's whereabouts. The inner pictures flashed to our descent into the laboratories to rescue the children and then our subsequent ascent into the school.

Ari had left us in the basement rooms, but anyone following my scent would arrive at the science classroom to find my discarded coat and a missing wolf, driven away in Sebastian's SUV. Shit! Zak had no idea that we were working together, he didn't know Adam was with us, he had no clue that Sebastian had helped us do so much including destroying the Evermore warehouse. To my brother, I was missing, and I knew what that feeling was like. For years I hadn't known where my brother was, but he had always kept tabs on me, until now. I slumped onto the sand burying my head in my arms and let the sobs wrack my body.

I was aware of someone standing behind me and was surprised to find Ethan kicking at the sand a few feet away from me.

'I'm sorry about your brother,' he said.

If I hadn't felt so desolate I might have laughed.

'No you're not.'

He chuckled and crouched down beside me.

'I'll never understand you, Mia, but I'm not totally heartless. Family is important and even though your brother is a freak, I get why you would care about him.'

I stared at him. In his own warped way I think he was trying to be nice, but nice wasn't what I needed right now.

'It's all my fault,' I said. 'Zak took the pack to Hood Academy to rescue *me*.'

If anything happened to him, Byron, or the other wolves, I'd never be able to forgive myself. I realised how foolish I'd been to leave without a word. I should have at least taken my phone with me so I could stay in touch with Cody. He must have been going out of his mind with worry. Cody was the rock I clung to when the rapids swirled around me and yet I'd left without saying a word. Ethan was right. I did turn my back on everyone.

A sob caught in my throat and I jumped up from the sand and swiped at the tears on my face.

'We need to go,' I said with more determination in my voice than I felt. 'I have to return home and fix the mess I've made.'

Ethan joined me as I ran back along the beach. Rushing back towards that small cottage on the seafront I felt a crushing sensation in my chest. What if I was too late?

THE SUV'S ENGINE hummed in the background as we said our goodbyes to Liam and the Somerset pack. I had decided to go on ahead instead of waiting for the pack to assemble. Liam assured us that if we needed their help, his pack would make their way to Nottingham and join us in the fight.

Evermore Pharmaceuticals needed to be stopped before any more children were harmed, or killed, but right now, Parker and the GA were the problem.

Adam and Elizabeth walked up to where I stood shaking hands with Liam and his wife, who nodded their greeting to the pair before moving off to speak with Sebastian.

'Are you sure you're not going to come with us?' After hearing about an Evermore delivery heading to the packs in Cornwall, Adam had decided to travel south and try to get his old school to help. It was at the Cornish Academy that Adam had met Miss Ross and formed a friendship that would see her call on him to help us.

I understood the need to help his old friends, both hunter and wolf, but I felt sad for Lizzie who had to say goodbye to her boyfriend once again.

'I need to see if there's anything I can do. Liam has called ahead and warned the packs to stay clear of the Evermore team, but if none of the alphas bring their children forward, I'm worried the academy will send a team out to force it on them.'

We'd started to hear similar stories trickling in over the past day or two, where the alpha had refused the cure and teams of soldiers had swept through their homes taking the children against their will. The incident with Ethan and the Somerset hunters wasn't an isolated occurrence and the packs needed all the help they could get.

Fights were breaking out all over the country as the packs began to rise up, but without any structure, these small skirmishes wouldn't make any difference. It was becoming clear that Parker had the entire resources of the GA at his disposal while using Evermore as a cover for his despicable plan. That meant he had access to weapons, funds, and hunters.

None of us had yet established if the GA were also involved. They were holding Hood Academy under review but Parker was smart; he could hide in plain sight if necessary, leading the GA into a game they weren't aware they were playing.

'With the new school term around the corner we can't risk the younger students getting caught up in a war,' Adam said. 'They're training to be hunters and will be brainwashed into believing that all the wolves need to die rather than keeping the peace. I need to try and make a difference.'

I understood exactly how Adam felt. The hunters' oath was clear; *to every pack, a cub is born. Unleash the hunter to protect and serve.* Protect and serve, not kill. Over time the true meaning of the academies had been lost somewhere. The role of the hunters was to protect their community from the wolves, not to seek them out and destroy them.

The origins of Hood Academy may have been to assist Queen Victoria in ridding the country of lycanthropy, but the modern teachings had been much more sympathetic in their dealings with the local packs.

Perhaps it was me, but I'd read Dr Neale's book at Sebastian's request and found the message of tolerance to be the stronger theme.

'I wish you didn't have to go,' Elizabeth said, wrapping her arms around Adam's waist and dropping her head on his chest.

'But I understand why you do. Just promise you'll stay safe.'

They kissed, and I averted my eyes, glancing out across the beach and the ocean beyond. I made a vow to return here when all this was over. Being by the sea made my heart soar and filled me with that sense of freedom that I'd longed for all my life.

Yes, when this mess was cleared up I'd be back.

'Time to go,' Sebastian called to us from the SUV, and we ambled over shaking hands with the assembled pack members as we went.

There was a sombre mood hanging in the air, mixed with anger, trepidation, and fear. It clung to me like a physical entity, a burden upon my shoulders.

Elizabeth slid into the back of the car, and I climbed in the front next to Sebastian, giving a final wave to Adam, Liam, and our new friends. Before Sebastian could pull out of the driveway, the back door swung wide and Ethan jumped in.

'What are you doing?' I snapped. I had little patience for the boy as it was, despite his attempts to comfort me on the beach, but the thought of a long road trip with him didn't fill me with joy.

'I'm coming with you,' he said clicking his seat belt into the clip. 'You're not leaving me with a bunch of wolves. I'm a hunter, and I belong with other hunters.' He gave me a sidelong glance as if that last comment wasn't fully meant to include me.

'We might not agree on certain things, Mia, but I can help you.'

I twisted around so I could look into his eyes.

'How can you help us? You don't even agree with what we're trying to do.'

He gave me a wide smile and I almost believed it was genuine.

'I'm a hunter, just like Elizabeth.' He jerked his thumb in Lizzie's direction and she rolled her eyes. 'I can fight and hunt.'

'You hunt werewolves, Ethan. That's who we're going to help. What does your oath-obsessed conscience say about that?'

He shrugged his shoulders and nestled down into the car seat. 'If I help you rescue your brother then maybe you can owe me. That hybrid power has to be good for something.'

'Oh, so now it's all about what I can do for you?' I could feel my pulse starting to throb as my anger and irritation grew. The kid was infuriating but I couldn't deny that an extra pair of hands would be welcome.

'Exactly. It's a win-win situation.'

I huffed and sat back in the seat.

'Do you think I could have my phone back now?' he added. 'I want to listen to my music while we're in the car.'

Glaring at him I dug his phone out of my pocket and tossed it at him. At least if he was listening to music he wouldn't spend the entire journey winding me up.

Sebastian caught my attention, and I rolled my eyes in an attempt to convey my unhappiness but acceptance of the situation. Luckily Sebastian got it and moved the car forward.

It didn't matter if Ethan came with us, or that Sebastian was driving us, I was going home to help my family, and that was the only thing that counted.

THE JOURNEY WAS subdued; Elizabeth buried her head in a book and Ethan plugged his earphones in, the muted sounds of some rock band echoing around the car.

'Did you manage to read that notebook about hybrids?' Sebastian broke the silence, pulling me out of my jumbled thoughts.

'Not all of it, I've only read the main references to hybrids, but it does sound similar to my situation.'

'Do you know who wrote it?'

I hadn't given it much thought if I was honest. The word hybrid had stood out for me like a neon marker and stripped away any curiosity.

'It was Dr Neale.'

'You mean Queen Victoria's werewolf hunter?'

'The very same. He was recruited by the crown to defend the country, but he was also a scientist and had a thirst for finding answers.'

'Hmm, bit like you then.'

Sebastian huffed, and I remembered his inability to express emotion faltered on occasion. His little huff was the equivalent to laughing out loud, something I'd adopted as a trait too, I realised.

My forehead crinkled as I drew my eyebrows together.

'What else do you have in common with an ancient hunter apart from both being the head of Hood Academy?'

'Do you remember the conversation we had when you first arrived at the academy? You commented on the cool stuff I'd collected.'

Pushing aside my amazement that Sebastian remembered any of our conversations, I did recall talking to him about the building and its impressive collection of old furniture and books. The place never felt cluttered; instead, it was safe, warm, and cosy. I'd remarked on this right before telling Sebastian I wanted to leave.

'Yes, I remember. You told me you'd inherited most of it.'

'That's right.' Sebastian's shoulders lifted as he mirrored my reaction. We both apparently appreciated the fact our conversations were memorable.

'Well, the academy and its contents were handed down the family line, passing from generation to generation. I'm one hunter in a very long line, and you, Mia, are part of that history.'

'I don't think I'm worthy of inheriting anything as I'm not a fully fledged hunter. In fact, I'm fairly certain that dear old Dr Neale would turn in his grave if he knew you were entertaining a hybrid in his precious academy!'

'That's where you're wrong, Mia. If you'd managed to read the notebook you'd have found some interesting information about our family line.'

'So why don't you tell me,' I urged, starting to lose patience in Sebastian's cryptic ramblings.

'Dr Neale was my great-great-great-granddad.'

My head spun as I processed what he was saying.

'You mean I'm descended from Queen Victoria's hunter?' I laughed. I laughed so loud it made Elizabeth jump and Ethan snarl at having his music interrupted.

'What's so funny about that?' Sebastian's face crumpled at my reaction.

'I'm sorry, but if Gramps knew about me, he'd excommunicate you for fraternising with a werewolf.'

Sebastian did huff at that.

'Everything is not always as it seems, Mia. Dr Neale wrote about the hunters' oath in 1862 when Ravenshood was overrun by wolves. He was a bit like Mr Parker at the time, adamant that the wolves were evil and desperate to destroy the packs. With money from the Crown, he opened Hood Academy in 1866 and began training those students who had come into contact with the wolves.'

'I remember, both you and Lizzie told me that to become a hunter you had to have seen a werewolf. Her sister didn't see what it was that attacked them, so Lizzie was the only one sent to Hood Academy.'

'Yes, there's some truth in that, but it's not altogether correct. I'm fairly sure Elizabeth's sister did see the werewolf, but her young mind wasn't open to the possibility of supernatural creatures being real. We recruit the believers because you can't help what you can't see.'

'Help? You've never wanted to help the wolves! You strapped Terry to a metal trolley and injected him with God knows what.' I could feel the trickle of anger dancing up my spine as I recalled finding my friend trapped in the school laboratories. 'You train the students to hunt and fight. I wasn't at Hood Academy for that long but what I saw during my time there told me you'd do everything in your power to hurt not help the packs.'

Sebastian shook his head, and for a moment I saw true sadness in his expression. I knew he was trying to turn it around and help us fix what was going on but was he really so delusional that he thought he hadn't done anything wrong?

'You're right,' he whispered. 'Dr Neale founded Hood Academy with the intention of destroying the local werewolves, but then he met a girl and fell in love.'

'Oh God, you're not going to get all mushy on me, are you?'

'He fell in love with a werewolf, Mia, like I did when I fell in love with your mother.'

Silence. Even Ethan's music seemed to lower in tone and pace.

'How could he? That would have gone against everything he believed in, and against the Queen's orders.'

'It appears love really can conquer all. The school became a sanctuary and a cover story. He married his sweetheart in secret, and they went on to have a child. A hybrid. The first hybrid.'

I felt like a bomb had gone off in my head; the noise was horrific. My jaw ached, and I realised with horror that my fangs had slid out. I covered them with my hand and prayed that the claws didn't shoot into view too.

'There have been three hybrids in the history of our family line, and you're one of them. The first two wrote about their experiences in that notebook you hold. Perhaps one day you can add your story.'

For the first time in a while, I was stumped for words. I had always had an answer for Sebastian, whether that was genuine or sarcastic, but this went beyond even my comprehension.

Three hybrids. I couldn't help but wonder what they had been like. Had they also felt like outsiders? Had they struggled to separate the parts of themselves that were wolf and hunter?

'Did they stay at Hood Academy?' I asked, relieved to find my teeth were normal again.

'I believe so. The first was Dr Neale's daughter, Emma. She was born in 1868. I don't think the next hybrid appeared until the 1950s when Mary was born.'

'So when you said we were rare you weren't kidding!'

Sebastian huffed again.

'There's certainly been a long time between each hybrid, but perhaps that shows us how the werewolf and hunter communities work.'

'I don't understand what you mean.'

'Our ancestor, Dr Neale, fell in love with a werewolf and got married, and they went on to have Emma, but it was over eighty years before another hunter and wolf would fall in love, marry, and produce a second hybrid offspring.'

'Then you came along and fell in love with my mum making number three, me!'

It had an air of the historical romance about it. Like all these pictures I had in my head were coated in a sepia wash or as if I was watching an old movie play out in my head.

'The hostility between the hunters and the packs has meant the oath taken by the new hunters has evolved over the years. It's this animosity that's gathered speed rather than the protection in the community that the oath was based on.'

'That's why you were trying to create the cure.' It was starting to make sense now. Sebastian's determination and drive to find a cure for lycanthropy wasn't done in malice, it was because he had loved my mother so much and wanted to make a better world for her.

There was a heavy weight in my chest as I thought about all the awful things I'd said to Sebastian over the last few months. I had called him a monster and walked away from him.

'I'm sorry,' I whispered reaching over to lay my hand over his on the steering wheel.

He turned his palm so he could squeeze my hand in return.

'You've got nothing to be sorry about, Mia. I did so many things wrong, and letting your mother down was my biggest failure. That's why I didn't want to make the same mistakes with you.'

I appreciated the sentiment even if he had gone about it in a barbaric manner, but I wondered what he was planning to do next.

'You said Dr Neale used the academy as a cover for his relationship with his werewolf wife. Were you doing the same?'

'In a way,' he said. 'I wanted to keep your mum safe, but we had to hide so much of our relationship from Frank, her pack, and the GA. Eventually, I had Mr Parker's threat hanging over my head, so instead of helping the local pack I ended up being the reason they were captured and tortured.'

I shook off my memory of finding Terry tied to the silver trolley in the basement, and hearing his screams when Felicity and her goons tortured him. Was she doing the same to Zak right now? If she knew he was my brother, I was certain she'd do more than torture him.

'Parker doesn't agree with your view of living in harmony with the packs.'

Sebastian exhaled. 'That's an understatement. Mr Parker's intense hatred of the wolves drives him to destroy the werewolf line. I thought I'd finally got through to him when he approached me about working with Evermore. He wanted to distribute the cure across the country to help the packs. I should have realised what he was really doing.'

'You're not the first person to be tricked, Sebastian. He was using you to create something that contained werewolf DNA so he could add his poison.'

'I should have known though. As head of Hood Academy, I was responsible for every life in that school. Every student was there to train and learn how to protect themselves. I allowed Mr Parker to pull me away from that mission.'

'I know I wasn't there for long, but even I saw how much the students loved it there. They learned so much, they laughed with their friends, and they were safe. You created that, Sebastian, and you shouldn't forget it.'

'Thank you, Mia. I appreciate your words. Unfortunately, it doesn't detract from the fact that I failed and the GA will no doubt strip me of everything I have.'

'Do the GA know what Parker's doing?' It was something I'd wanted to know from the beginning. We all wondered if their sudden appearance was coincidental, but most of us thought not.

Sebastian shook his head. 'I honestly don't know. The GA are reviewing the school after recent events and might grant Mr Parker full headship, but I don't know if they are aware of the links to Evermore, or what Mr Parker has planned for the packs.'

A shudder ran up my spine as I thought about Parker's plans. With help from his evil pharmaceutical company, he had managed to sweep across half of England dishing out his poison. How many had died? How many young children were forced to turn before they were old enough to cope with the pain and hunger? I felt sick thinking about it.

I looked down at the notebook still in my hand. Everything I needed to know about being a hybrid was within these pages. If being half hunter and half wolf could help my brother and the pack then it was time to embrace my unique abilities.

We had a big fight ahead of us, not just with the GA and trying to free our friends, but stopping Parker and Evermore Pharmaceuticals before more wolves died.

I flipped open the book. It was time to find out who I really was.

OATH KEEPER

TEN

The Mills farm was in chaos when we pulled up in the driveway. I saw Terry through the kitchen window and the weight lifted from my shoulders knowing at least one of my friends was safe.

The first thing I saw when walking in through the old wooden door was the kitchen table covered with blueprints of Hood Academy and maps of the local area interspersed with numerous cups of coffee. How long had everyone been sitting at this table?

'Mia!' Terry was out of his chair and at my side in seconds. His embrace almost took my breath away as he squeezed me tight. 'We were all so worried. Ari arrived with a ton of kids and babbled something about you and Lizzie snooping around the school.'

Elizabeth came in behind me and Terry released his grip on me and circled her in an equally tight embrace.

'We're so sorry,' I said, raising my voice to include everyone gathered in the small kitchen. 'We never meant to worry you. After finding the children and sending Ari back here, we found information about the serum and had to leave to investigate it further. I should have called. I should have let you know we were safe...'

My voice trailed off as I spotted Cody in the doorway. Dark smudges ringed his glazed-over eyes, and he rubbed at his upper arm as if to drive away a chill. I rushed to him, and he scooped me up burying his face in my long hair.

The sound of his sobs ripped a hole in my heart that I didn't think I'd ever recover from.

'I'm so sorry,' I whispered into his ear, trailing kisses along his cheek and blotting the tears that lingered on his face. 'I'll never leave you again.'

He brought his lips to mine and kissed me deeply, oblivious to the watchful eyes of the pack, who began shuffling and moving about in a bid to avoid our intimate exchange.

The sudden silence in the room tore Cody and me apart, and I turned to see what had muted the pack. Sebastian stood in the doorway clutching the files we'd taken from Parker's desk drawer. Terry's shoulders tensed at the sight of the man responsible for his incarceration and torture.

'What the hell are you doing here?' It was Cody who spoke, stunning me with the venom that dripped from his words. I took a step backward and released my grip on him.

'Sebastian's with us. He's been really helpful to our cause, to *your* cause.'

'That man is only out to help himself; he doesn't give a shit about the wolves.'

'No, you're wrong. He helped me and Lizzie burn down the Evermore distribution centre, and he saved the lives of three young wolves in Somerset. He's on our side.'

I looked around at the faces of Zak's pack. Bared teeth, crossed arms, and angry eyes greeted me. They weren't going to accept Sebastian's help without an argument, and part of me understood that. It had taken an epic journey to be able to start to bond with the man myself, and he was my own flesh and blood. I was expecting a miracle if I wanted them to open their home and hearts to him.

I took the files from Sebastian and placed them on the table in front of the pack.

'We have evidence that Parker has modified Sebastian's serum, which is what's causing the children to turn or die. He plans to wipe out the werewolf gene by destroying your kids.'

There was a rumbling of conversation as the files and their contents spilled out across the table.

'If *he* hadn't created the serum in the first place none of this would have happened.'

Sebastian rolled his shoulders and took a step forward, further inside the danger zone.

'I understand your animosity,' he said, his voice clear and strong. 'My intentions have always been for the good of the werewolf community. I loved a wolf and would have done anything to keep her safe, but my work has been mutilated by a man hell-bent on destroying all of you.'

'It's true,' I said standing at Sebastian's side. 'Parker is behind Evermore Pharmaceuticals, and it's him who's sent the doctors out into our community with the promise of a cure. No one could have known what he was planning. Even Sebastian thought it was the right serum being sent out to the packs.'

'Are you telling me that you've developed a cure for lycanthropy?' Terry stood at the head of the table, in Zak's spot, standing in for his alpha who was captive at Sebastian's old school. How the wolves hadn't ripped my father's throat out already amazed me.

'Yes, that's exactly what I'm telling you. It will only work on the young to avoid them turning, I haven't been able to create a cure for fully fledged wolves, and I think that's a fool's errand that I can't continue.'

Sebastian let the information sink in before going on. 'My serum was tampered with, and I suspect Parker's staff at Evermore had something to do with that. It explains why he kept me working in the school laboratories instead of at the central pharmaceutical facility.'

'What have the GA got to do with it?' One of the visiting pack members asked the question that many of us were desperate to know the answer to.

'I don't believe they've got anything to do with it,' Sebastian answered. 'I don't even think they know Mr Parker is connected to Evermore Pharmaceuticals. The GA are at Hood Academy to review my recent misdemeanours.'

'You mean they're here to find out why you captured and tortured us and tried to kill your own daughter,' Terry added.

Sebastian hung his head, and I felt a mix of anger and loyalty towards my friend.

'Leave him alone,' I said. 'Yes, he messed up, big time, but he's here to help us get Zak, Byron, and the others back. He knows Hood Academy better than any of us. Let him help.'

I HADN'T EXPECTED to be banished from the kitchen with Sebastian in tow. In all fairness, they'd done it so they could discuss our rescue plan in private, but I was fuming at Terry for kicking me out of the inner circle.

Sebastian had taken himself off to sit in his SUV for safety and Elizabeth was checking in on Ari. I'd almost forgotten about our hunter guest until Ethan sauntered over to where I was sitting on the bonnet of a car in the driveway.

'When I came with you I thought you'd be taking me to Hood Academy, not to another wolf den.' He crossed his arms over his chest and settled his dark gaze on me. 'You do know that your hairy friends have been growling at me ever since I arrived.'

'It's a pit stop, we'll be heading to the academy soon enough, although you might not want to join us for that trip.'

'Yeah, I gathered from the raised voices that your pets were planning to attack the school.'

'It's not an attack,' I snapped, annoyed at both his assumptions and disrespect for my pack. 'The GA are holding some of our friends, and the alpha, and we want to get them back.'

He unfolded his arms and leaned against the car watching me with a predatory glance that made me feel uncomfortable. It was the kind of look that made your skin crawl. So far, the infuriating hunter had tagged along with a half-hearted offer of help, but I didn't know if I should trust Ethan yet. He was arrogant but loyal to the hunters' oath and in my eyes that made him unpredictable.

'You think you're going to get past the GA? Jeez, you're stupider than you look.'

I jumped off the car and stood nose to nose with the hunter.

'What's your problem with me, Ethan?'

He snarled, actually snarled, and I had to pull on all my reserves not to slap him hard across his smarmy face.

'You say you're half hunter, but you live with wolves. It's like I told you in Somerset, you could never understand the hunters' oath if you don't respect it enough to honour it.'

I was speechless. I'd come to expect a personal attack about my claws or living with a pack, but Ethan still sounded genuinely angry that I'd not upheld the oath.

'I took the oath with every intention of being a hunter, but a lot of stuff happened that was out of my control. Other people weren't happy about me being at the academy, and it made it hard.'

'Oh, my heart bleeds for you. So what, Felicity goes all crazy bitch on you, and you decide to turn to the wolves?'

I took a step back and studied the boy properly for the first time. He was my age with pale skin, which made his dark hair stand out even more. A dusting of pimples on his chin told me he'd recently started shaving and it had irritated his skin. At about five foot ten he was a few inches taller than me, and it annoyed me that I had to look up at him.

'How do you know about Felicity?' Suspicion bubbled in my gut as I waited for his answer.

'Everyone knows about Felicity, she's a legend among the academies.'

I huffed and rolled my eyes. 'A legend! The girl's a freak.'

'Maybe, but she's still badass.'

I laughed out loud, and Ethan flinched at the sudden outburst.

'Did you also hear that I beat her at the last assessment? Thrashed her to take the gold medal and humiliated her in front of her precious daddy.'

There was the briefest spark of appreciation in Ethan's expression before he shrugged and walked away.

'Perhaps Hood Academy has two legends then,' he called over his shoulder.

Was that a compliment? Maybe there was hope for the hunter after all.

TERRY CAME AND found me a little while later with the news that our rescue attempt would happen after dark.

'I suppose if I asked you to stay here you wouldn't listen,' said Terry.

'You suppose right, it's my brother that's in trouble, and I'm going to help save him.'

'Hmm, thought as much. I've asked Lizzie to stay and watch the kids, and your weird friend Ethan has offered to help us too.'

'He's not my friend, but I appreciate that he's trying to help. What about Sebastian?'

Terry ran his fingers through his hair and in that moment he reminded me so much of Zak. Without my brother and Byron around it fell on Terry to hold the pack together.

He'd never struck me as the sort to relish leadership. Terry was the funny one, the caring one, the loyal, strong, and daring one. What if it all went horribly wrong and we couldn't get Zak back? Would Terry snap under the pressure?

'I think it's best if Sebastian comes with us. He could be a distraction for the GA if we come into contact with any of them.'

'You mean a sacrifice.'

Terry gave a short nod.

'Do you know where they're holding Zak and the others?'

'We've got our suspicions. The laboratories are the logical choice, but there's also the animal cages at the back of the property. If they have them heavily guarded, it'll be difficult to set them free no matter where they are.'

'We'll get him back, Terry,' I said linking my arm into his. 'We'll get them all back.'

SHELLEY WILSON

ELEVEN

I felt like I was spending more time at Hood Academy recently than I ever did when I was a student. First, there was the incident with Ari, then finding Sebastian on the school's extensive grounds, rescuing Elizabeth, returning to find the captive children, and now another rescue attempt to save my brother and the pack members.

During the few short months I'd been at Hood Academy I'd run away three times. There was an irony in there somewhere. Running from the academy when I was a student and now returning to the academy when I was supposed to be a pack member. Maybe Ethan was right. Perhaps if I'd been more dedicated to upholding the hunters' oath, I wouldn't feel so displaced.

The pack moved through the forest towards the back of the school, approaching the animal cages first to see if this was where our family and friends were being held. We were all still in human form having decided this was the best way to track and rescue our friends. It meant walking at a slower pace, but I understood how it would be difficult to sneak six huge wolves through the back door. I walked with Sebastian as Terry had given me the task of looking after my father. Ethan had also been placed in my 'keep them out of the pack's way' group. I hoped Terry understood why I had to give Sebastian a chance. He was my biological father as well as being the psycho scientist we'd got to know too well. If there was any hope that I could carve some kind of relationship out of all this mess, then I was willing to try.

Through the inky blackness of the forest, I could see the pack creeping forward, their human shapes melting into the trees with ease. If the GA discovered us, there was a high probability that each of the pack members would turn to protect themselves.

Cody had told me more about the turn after I discovered that werewolves were real. He explained how they always turned on a full moon but other than that they remained human unless attacked. Felicity and her goons beat Cody when he'd come to rescue me. When he turned, I couldn't look away. It was horrific and beautiful at the same time. Snapping bones, shifting limbs, and gut-wrenching screams. No wonder Sebastian had made the cure. Who would want that for their children?

'Wait,' Terry hissed back at us, and we halted our steps.

Through the overhanging branches I could see the twinkling lights of Hood Academy. The GA would be located in one specific area. Sebastian told us that any reviews they had done in the past were carried out from the library, which was on the west side of the building. If we could contain them in one place, it would make it easier for the scouts to search for Zak and Byron.

A runner returned to Terry's side. Would we be heading to the animal cages or had the GA chosen to lock our friends up in the laboratories? Terry waved his hand in the air, and we all moved off as one. The laboratories it was then.

As we reached the treeline, I spotted the bright lights illuminating the dormitory rooms. Why weren't they still in darkness? The students weren't due to start the new term for another week. I tuned into my senses and listened. Through the wind and drizzle, I heard the playful tones of young girls laughing and talking. Panic flooded my entire body, and my hands began shaking. I looked over at Ethan with wide eyes and saw the realisation spread across his face.

'Stop!' He turned towards the pack, attracting Terry's attention with a frantic wave of his arms. 'There are students here.'

Terry appraised the building, casting his eyes up to the second and third floors where silhouettes of students moved across the glass.

'It doesn't change anything.' Terry waved the pack forward.

I watched helplessly as Terry, Cody, and the other pack members crossed the lawns and made their way to the back door, which led to the kitchens. Sebastian had told them it would be the easiest access point, but if the students were back, that meant the kitchen staff would be too.

'Are you going to let them attack students?' Ethan hissed. 'Is this what being a hybrid is all about?'

Panic filled my chest as I struggled with my dual personalities. We had to rescue Zak and the others, but I also had a duty to protect the girls inside.

'Come on you two!' I grabbed Sebastian's hand and dragged him along with me as I sprinted after the wolves with Ethan matching my pace.

I pushed past the assembled pack until I reached Terry's side. He had a crowbar wedged into the kitchen doorframe ready to break in.

'Let me go in first,' I said, unable to mask the desperation in my voice. 'I can keep to the shadows and get an idea of where everyone is. If anyone does see me, they'll think I'm another student. That's got to be better than a werewolf pack bursting into a school full of hunters.'

I could see Terry thinking over his options. He was used to following orders not giving them. Eventually, he nodded his consent, and I breathed a sigh of relief.

'Okay, I need two teams. Ethan, I want you to check out the nurse's office that Lizzie told us about in case they used that entrance. Mia will go this way. I don't want *either* of you to engage with the people inside. We don't need the students seeing you and getting distressed. Find out where Zak is and then get back here as fast as you can.'

Ethan shot off into the night and I felt a strange sense of satisfaction that he was working with us.

Before I could enter the kitchen door Terry grabbed my wrist.

'Mia, I want Cody to go with you as backup.'

I opened my mouth to complain but he held his hand up to stop me.

'It's not because I don't trust you,' he said softly. 'I'd just feel happier if someone had your back. He can stay hidden in the doorway but I want him close to you. Zak would never forgive me if anything happened to you.'

I understood, and instead of getting argumentative with him I smiled and squeezed his arm. 'You need to stay in the treeline,' I said. 'If the students are here that means the staff will be milling about too and I wouldn't want the cook to stumble across you lot in her backyard.'

Terry grinned at me in the way he used to, full of the boyish charm that had been so endearing when we'd first met. I needed to find my brother so everyone could be who they were meant to be, me included.

THE DINING HALL was in darkness; we'd missed the dinner rush, and the staff had fortunately packed up and left. The main entrance hall was on the other side of the dining room through the closed glass door. I could see the light blazing and hear murmured voices. Directly opposite this room was Sebastian's office, or rather Parker's office as he now held the position of headmaster.

'We have to go through that door into the main building,' I told Cody who was tailing me. 'But we need to wait until whoever's out there has left or they'll see us.'

I couldn't remember if this door handle squealed like some of the older ones in the school. I gripped it in my sweaty palm, and I prayed that opening this door wouldn't blow our entire mission.

It twisted easily, and I tugged it open a fraction. The main entrance hall was exactly how I remembered it. Squishy sofas circled the walls, interspersed with chunky mahogany furniture. The lamps were lit, but there were no students lounging there this evening. The voices I'd heard earlier were coming from Parker's room where the office door was ajar. I couldn't help the roll of my gut on recognising Felicity's voice.

'What if the GA let them go, Daddy?'

'They're foolish enough to do something like that. Those damn idiots couldn't organise a bake sale. We've worked too hard for these morons to risk it all.'

'I thought they would have gone by now. Surely they know you're the best person for the headmaster's job instead of that imbecilic wolf lover, Sebastian.'

I bristled at her words and felt Cody's fingers intertwine with my free hand. His warmth gave me the strength I needed.

'Yes, I thought that bringing the students back early might have encouraged them to leave, but no matter,' Parker said. 'Fortunately, my sweet child, the GA are as clueless about my dealings with Evermore Pharmaceuticals as they are about dealing with vermin wolves. They prance around *my* school demanding evidence of Sebastian's ill-advised experiments as if I were the guilty one.'

Felicity's giggle echoed around the rooms. 'You *are* guilty, Daddy.'

Parker's booming laughter mingled with his daughter's as they relished in the downfall of my father.

'My hands are clean, pumpkin. Only Sebastian knows of my involvement with his creation, and a single threat against the life of his wolf lover was enough to convince him to stay quiet.'

'Didn't that cow die anyway?'

'Ah yes, but by whose hand? Sometimes we need to intervene when it's for the good of the hunters' oath.'

Felicity's wild laughter tore through my chest like a bullet. The pain in my heart threatened to rip me apart, and I couldn't stop myself from shaking violently. Cody wrapped his muscular arms around me, sensing my horror. Sebastian believed he had killed my mother, the love of his life. *I* had believed he had killed my mother, as did everyone else, but it was a lie. Parker had interfered with Sebastian's experiments just as he was doing now.

I could barely hear their words as the screaming in my head intensified. Cody clung to me, possibly fearing that I might lose it and murder everyone in my way.

'It's all worked out for the best, my darling daughter. The GA will conclude that Sebastian set up a private venture in conjunction with Evermore to wipe out the wolves. Being a caring parent and governor, I stepped in to look after the interests of the academy and uphold the oath, and if I can time it right, everyone will believe that when his experiment went horribly wrong, he was driven to destroy all the evidence. If they believe Dr Roberts capable of such atrocities as murdering young wolves and silencing their families as they grieve for their cubs then they'll end him, and his filthy bloodline.'

Cody was struggling to keep me in his grasp. My fangs had emerged, and my claws were fully extracted, but I could feel something else, something new happening to my body. The muscles beneath my skin rippled with energy and my blood boiled.

A searing pain shot down my spine as I lurched forward out of Cody's arms. My legs buckled under me and I hit the floor. I braced myself against the hard surface as my claws stretched out before me. The pain screeched through my entire body, and I watched partly in horror and partly in awe as my hands pulsed and twitched. My right leg snapped backward, the bone breaking and moulding into another shape as I wept at the agony. The left leg followed. I'd never known such torture. Even the beatings Frank had subjected me to were nothing compared to this.

I was aware of movement all around me. Cody had alerted the pack. His soft voice lulled me from somewhere that seemed far away. Terry's strong tones carried an authority I'd never heard before, and I tried to remember how to speak. I wanted to communicate with my friends. I needed to scream for them to help me.

I opened my mouth and felt my jaw rip as it widened beyond any reasonable boundary. More fangs slid into place bursting through my gums with terrific force. My shoulders rounded and snapped apart as my spine buckled and twisted.

Sweat poured from me in waves and the nausea frightened me. I strained against the urge to scream as the pain reverberated through my bones. Any cry would attract attention that we didn't need. If it was any consolation, I knew I wasn't alone. The wolves had joined me in the dining hall as a measure of support, but I wasn't sure I relished having an audience.

When would it end? I realised the enormity of what I was going through. I was turning into a werewolf, a fully fledged wolf. No more hybrid fangs and cute claws, this was serious shit. Watching Cody turn all those months ago had been bad enough, I would have done anything to help him as he cried out in pain, but now he was forced to watch me, unable to offer anything but his soft words of comfort.

My hands were no longer hands; instead I could see huge paws covered in silky brown fur. My arms snapped into place allowing me to lift myself off the floor. I could feel the power in my limbs as I rose from the ground. I flung my head back as my spine contorted and manoeuvred into another position. Then it was done. Over. I was a wolf.

I rose higher, my arms and legs settling into position as I looked around the room for the first time. My eyes focused differently. I could see figures all around me, but it was harder to pick out who was who. I sniffed and instantly recognised Cody's scent.

'Don't be afraid, Mia. I'm here with you.'

I wasn't afraid. For the first time in my life, I felt in control. A strength vibrated through me that I had only ever dreamed of. Images of Frank rolled across my mind. Him towering over me with that grotesque snarl before wrapping his fingers around my throat, his heavy boot as it connected with my body. All the times he had hurt me. Suddenly I understood how easy it had been for Zak to rip out his throat. Right here, right now, I knew I could do the same.

My breathing was slow and steady as I waited for whatever came next. The pack remained in their human form and whispered to each other. I could almost taste their energy.

'Parker and his daughter are behind everything,' Cody explained. 'We overheard it all. The GA has nothing to do with the murders; it's all Parker.'

'Then we take out the main threat, rescue our pack, and get the hell out of here before...' Terry's voice trailed off as he glanced over his shoulder at me. His scent was strong and musty, but there was also an edge to it, a rippling of fear that rolled off him in waves. Was he afraid of me, or of what I might do?

Parker's voice interrupted my thoughts as he spoke to his daughter.

'I think the time's come to finish this little project, don't you? I'll keep the GA occupied while you go down to the lab. Here, this is Sebastian's lab coat. Leave it behind for the GA to find but make sure you don't leave any of the filthy wolves alive. I want them *all* dead.'

I heard Felicity leave the headmaster's office and enter the stockroom where the secret entrance to the laboratories was. I'd followed the redhead into that room before, but this time I wasn't going to be trembling in the shadows.

The growl rumbled up from the back of my throat as I edged towards the door.

Cody stood in front of me with his hands held high in the air. 'If you follow her, Mia, you'll kill her, and I don't want that for you.'

I bared my teeth, and his arms lowered.

'Let her save her brother,' Sebastian said stepping out of the darkness so I could see his shape. I sniffed the air and memorised his scent. It was slightly spicy, like a grown-up's aftershave mixed with coffee beans. 'For the good of your pack we have to trust that she can control her actions. I'll find the GA and let them know what's been happening.'

'If the GA see you they'll arrest you on sight,' Terry said.

'I know, and I probably deserve it, but if it gives you the time to rescue your friends and get free of this place, then it's worth the sacrifice.'

I saw Terry extend his hand in offering to Sebastian who took it gratefully. Maybe there was hope for my father yet.

'Okay, let's do this.'

TWELVE

ody hadn't left my side, and for that I was thankful. I needed his support more than ever as I took my first steps as a wolf.

The storeroom was more difficult to navigate since I was the size of a small horse, but I made it through and led the pack down the stone stairs to the basement rooms. Terry and a few others went first, creeping down the steps in silence. I followed with Cody at my back.

The muffled sounds of a struggle travelled along the corridor of rooms, and I urged Terry on. Felicity had barged through every door leaving them ajar in her eagerness to inflict pain and death on the captives. Her poisonous scent coated everything she'd touched.

'You don't have to do this!' Someone cried out in pain.

It was Byron, and the anguish in his tone pierced my heart.

As one we rushed forward bursting into the next room as Felicity held a dagger over Byron's heart. She jumped back from the table, holding the blade at arm's length assessing her assailants. Her widening eyes surveyed the room until that calculated look she was so well known for settled on her face. She took in the human forms of the pack, as if filing their images away for the future when she would hunt them down one by one.

I wasn't going to let that happen, and I relished the shock on her face as I entered the room, my huge paws padding along the floor leaving tiny clouds of dust. Standing to my full height, I growled at her. Even Byron's eyes widened. Cody stood by my side, and I felt the change in Felicity as she put the pieces together.

'Wolf girl,' she hissed. 'You've managed to turn, I see, and here was me thinking you couldn't do anything right.' She brushed her fingers along her throat and the raw scar left behind after our last fight.

'We're here to take our pack,' Cody spoke up, his voice cold and hard.

Felicity waved her dagger in Cody's direction. 'You're the one who nearly killed me in the woods that night, saving your girl.' She moved closer and the pack tensed as one.

'I must admit, Mia, he's cute, for a wolf. I can see why you'd let him slobber all over you.' She winked at Cody and circled back round to where Byron lay strapped to the metal trolley. 'Unfortunately, it's a hunter's responsibility to uphold the oath and rid the world of vermin like you, no matter how cute.'

The pack inched forward circling either side of Felicity who waved the dagger in front of her.

'Stay back!' she screamed, thrusting the blade towards Terry who froze. 'Don't take another step or your friend here dies.'

'You're outnumbered,' said Terry holding his hands out. 'You can't kill all of us.'

Her eyes flashed with anger as she glared from one person to the next registering Terry's words and realising she had already lost.

'I don't have to kill you all,' she spat, that glint in her eye like a warning light to anyone who stepped in her way. 'I only have to kill one of you.'

In one fluid movement she plunged the knife into Byron's gut, blood spurting in all directions as he screamed out in agony. The pack scattered, grabbing for the redhead as she skirted past them and disappeared through the next door along.

'Cut him loose,' Terry shouted. 'Get him out of here.'

Two of the pack rushed to help Byron, who coughed and spluttered from the table. Terry was in pursuit of Felicity before they'd cut the first bond.

I lurched forward almost knocking Cody off his feet as he darted after his friend.

The three of us pushed forward until we hit the last room. This was the same room where Sebastian had kept the children that Elizabeth, Ari, and I had rescued. Instead of kids, the room now held five men. I burst through the door and saw Felicity heading straight for Zak with the blood-stained blade in her hand.

The roar that erupted from my throat silenced the room. Even Felicity stopped and spun around, having the sense not to turn her back on me.

I padded forward never once taking my eyes off my nemesis. Her scent was overwhelming but Sebastian had believed in me. He thought I was capable of controlling my emotions and not killing another human, however evil they might be. I wanted that to be true. Underneath this powerful form, I was just a girl. Granted, I wasn't the same girl I used to be, I'd changed, grown harder, tougher, and more resilient, but I was still just a teenager with hopes and dreams that didn't include taking another life.

Within seconds Terry and Cody had freed our friends, and I had the pack at my back. Zak stood at my shoulder, his dark hair curling up at the nape of his neck. Right now, he didn't look like an alpha, he looked like my big brother.

'You've lost this fight, Felicity. The GA will make sure that because of your actions and cruelty you'll be stripped of your hunters' oath and sent back into the hole you wormed your way out of.'

'Tut, tut, Zak, you should know better than that. My daddy will have the GA eating out of his hand before you even make it to the trees. I'll be able to watch you die at the hands of the agency who'll never know how close we came to wiping your filthy species off this earth.'

'Your threats don't work on me, little girl, you're the most pathetic excuse for a hunter I've ever seen.'

Felicity snarled at my brother, the snide remark at her expense clearly not sitting well with her.

'In fact, once the GA discover what you and your father have been up to, I'm pretty certain you'll be locked away for good.'

'Don't they lock failed hunters up with the murderous wolves?' Terry teased. 'Yeah, I'm sure I heard that somewhere. The kids who don't cut it as a hunter are fed to the prey they tried so hard to destroy.'

'You're all monsters!' Felicity screamed, her eyes sparking with an inner fire. She wasn't going to give up easily.

She swiped at a stack of boxes with the Evermore logo on the side. They crashed to the floor at my feet, and the contents spilled out: hundreds of silver vials like the ones we'd found earlier containing Parker's evil serum. I lifted my paw and pounded at the tubes, smashing the casing and smearing the toxic green liquid across the stone floor.

The door leading back towards the nurse's office burst open, and Ethan lurched through holding his wooden staff. Felicity jumped away from him keeping a safe distance between the new arrival and the gathered pack. Ethan surveyed the room, only lingering on my wolf form for a few seconds.

'You need to leave,' he said. 'The GA are crawling all over the grounds looking for her.' He jerked his thumb at Felicity, and I felt a small tug of satisfaction.

'Who the hell are you?' Zak's voice was menacing as he looked over the hunter.

'It's fine,' Terry said. 'He's a friend of Mia's. Travelled up with her from Somerset yesterday. He's on our side.'

Zak didn't look convinced, but I was in no position to defend Ethan as the only sounds I could make were grunts and growls. I had to hope my brother believed Terry.

'Fine, let's go.' Zak gave a nod of his head. 'We'll leave Miss Parker to her fate.'

One by one the pack exited the room heading for the nurse's office and the safety of the trees beyond. I stalked forward baring my teeth at Felicity as I drew up next to her. She flinched away from me. Cody slapped Ethan on the shoulder in thanks and walked away. I didn't want Ethan getting caught up in this and waited for him to leave so I could protect him from any last-ditch attempt Felicity might make at attacking us.

As I reached the door, I saw the briefest of exchanges between the two hunters. Not a look of fear or revulsion but one of camaraderie. I watched Ethan pull his phone out and tap at the keys. Within seconds Felicity's mobile sang with the notification of a message received. She tapped the screen and smiled across at Ethan, blowing him a kiss. The chill of dread slid down my contorted spine as I worked out far too late that Ethan had fooled us all. He'd tricked me into returning his phone, and now I realised my error. He'd been in contact with my nemesis all along.

In one fluid motion, Felicity threw her dagger at me, and I roared as it struck me in the shoulder. She spun away, rolling across the floor to grasp at the remaining syringes. Ethan swung his staff around to smash into the exposed region of my head. I lurched to the side, momentarily stunned. In my clumsiness, I knocked the door closed, and as I lay on the floor trying to stop the world from spinning away, I noticed I was blocking the exit and preventing Cody and my brother from getting in to help me.

'Time to die, wolf girl,' Felicity spat the words at me as she flung the syringe at Ethan who caught it and brought it down hard on my leg. I felt the sharp sting as the needle broke through my skin and the rush of panic as he pumped the toxic contents into my system.

No! I wasn't ready to die.

My reaction was immediate. I began convulsing in the same way as the children we'd found in the Somerset woods. Sebastian had saved them with his tonics. I needed Sebastian. I needed my dad.

Felicity's shrill laughter snapped me back to the moment. She was draped over Ethan stroking his hair and kissing his cheek. The smarmy grin I'd always wanted to wipe off his face was the only thing I could see. At that moment everything became clear.

If it was my time to die, then I wasn't going alone. Zak had killed for me when he'd killed the bully who terrorised my childhood. So I could kill for him, for Cody, Terry, and Byron, for the pack, and my friends, for Ari and her sister. I would kill for all of them.

I rode the next wave of convulsions then summoned all my wolf healing to protect me from the toxins invading my system. Neither hunter was expecting my strike as I launched from the floor claws extended. I slashed out at Felicity, knocking her off balance before digging my claws into Ethan's flesh. I felt the warmth of his blood as my nails dragged across his throat. His eyes grew wide in horror as he pitched to his knees clutching at the gash in his neck where his life force was draining away. He stared at me in shock and I realised with some satisfaction that he had underestimated me. Felicity screamed as the door burst open behind me.

'You killed him,' she shrieked.

Her hysteria fed my rage and I growled, readying myself to pounce when another snarl filled the air. It was a sound I'd heard before and one I couldn't ignore. It was the call of my alpha.

Zak stood behind me in his wolf form, his immense size filling the doorframe. He growled at me again, and I dropped my head in submission.

Felicity's screams mingled with my brother's gentle persuasions as I stumbled from the room struggling against the rising convulsions again. The last thing I saw was the redhead cradling Ethan's lifeless body in her arms.

'I will find you, wolf girl,' she ranted, 'and I will kill you.'

The door slammed shut, and she was gone. Zak led me up and out onto the car park where Terry was waiting. They herded me into the forest where I collapsed as the toxic serum burnt through my organs. The spasms rocked my body like a child shaking her rag doll. My bones creaked and groaned as I returned to my human form, and the searing pain in my joints dulled as the damp forest floor soothed me. Cody rushed to my side ripping the syringe from my leg and throwing a blanket around my naked frame.

'We need to get her away from the academy,' he said, a thread of panic in his voice.

'She needs Sebastian,' Terry said.

I wanted to agree with him, tell him that's exactly what I needed but I couldn't form the right words. I was delirious, and anything that came out of my mouth would sound like gibberish. My skin was on fire, and sweat trickled down the side of my face. Cody scooped me up from the floor and cradled me close to his chest. The heat was too much, and I felt like I was being burnt at the stake. I wriggled and moaned, and I knew he thought it was the serum doing its job, but I couldn't tell him that he was killing me with kindness.

A noise up ahead put everyone on high alert, and I felt Cody shudder as he tried to prevent himself from turning.

Somehow, I knew he was willing himself to stay human so that he could hold and protect me.

'It's okay, it's Sebastian,' someone called out, the voices travelling back to where we stood. Sebastian was making his way through the trees, heading in our direction.

'Where is she?' His face filled my vision, which swam as I tried to focus. He lifted my eyelid and shone a light on me. I tried to flinch away, but Cody held me steady.

'We need to get her home. Follow me, the academy minibus is behind the school and the keys are always left in it.'

Cody jostled me back and forth as he hurried after Sebastian and bundled me into one of the seats. The engine started, and the vibrations carried through the metal and into my very soul. Everything hurt. The entire journey was torturous as I bounced around in the bus. Cody tried to soothe me as Sebastian drove like a maniac through endless dark lanes.

He finally stopped and I retched, first on the floor of the minibus and then again on the driveway.

'Quickly, get her inside.'

I looked up at the building ahead of us as Cody nestled me against his chest, the blanket tucked around my body. This place was unfamiliar. The stone cottage gleamed as we hurried through the front door. There was a cosy feel to the entrance hall with its flagstone floors, but I didn't get to see much as they rushed me through to a bedroom at the back of the cottage. Cody manoeuvred me into bed making sure I was covered up and kissing my burning forehead.

'What can I do to help?' he asked as Sebastian rolled up his sleeves and set to work unrolling a cloth with an assortment of vials and potions on it.

'Pray for her,' he said. 'The serum was only ever intended for a young child with the wolf gene. The modifications that Evermore made have mutated the strain so that the host gets pure poison. In a wolf child, this will accelerate the turning process as the body tries to heal and protect itself. By rights, all the children should die, but some of them have been able to resist.'

'How can they resist it?'

'I've only managed to look at some of the files so I'd need to do proper tests, but my early findings show that the children who survive have hunter DNA as well as wolf.'

'How is that possible?'

'I believe the barriers between the hunters and the wolves have been changing for some time, but clearly nobody dares talk about it. The horror of what Mr Parker has done might shine a light on a new era, Cody. One that you and Mia are already a part of.'

'What does it mean for Mia? She turned, Sebastian. I mean, fully turned.'

'Hmm, I know, but I'm not sure what will happen now. She was a hybrid with the strength of a hunter and the healing power of a wolf, but now...' He shook his head. 'I never stabilised the serum to cure lycanthropy, I only ended up killing her mother.'

I groaned and tried to speak. He had to know that it wasn't his fault, but I was slipping in and out of consciousness. The ceiling danced above me and joined hands with the walls. They spun together like they were dancing around a maypole. I thrashed my head from side to side trying to stop the whirling, but it didn't help. Cody's blonde hair filled my vision as he leaned over me, dragging a damp cloth across my forehead.

I willed him to tell Sebastian that he wasn't the one to kill my mother. I wanted to shout it out loud, so the entire world knew my father wasn't an evil man.

I wanted to, but the world was slipping away. Darkness played at the edges of my mind, creeping forward like a game of hide and seek. I felt the sharp scratch of a needle in my arm and hoped that whatever Sebastian was doing would work and bring me back.

The darkness grew, and the voices of my father and boy-friend became fainter. I felt like I was travelling down a long tunnel and there was no way back.

Somewhere in the blackness of this passageway, I could hear my friends. Elizabeth, Terry, and even Miss Ross. They whispered, but I was comforted to know they were there, somewhere.

Before I drifted off into sleep that might very well be eternal, I heard my brother's voice, clear and bright like he was standing right next to me.

'Come back to me, little sis,' he said. 'Come back to me.'

THIRTEEN

T hrough the cottage window I could see the blue sky and noticed the leaves on the treetops were starting to turn. The
oranges, reds, and yellows of autumn approached and with
them a new school term at Hood Academy.

I'd been lying in this bed for days as Sebastian worked hard to
stabilise the poison that pulsed through my body. When I wasn't
hallucinating, I was vomiting, and when that was done, I'd start
convulsing. It was a cycle that never seemed to end.

Elizabeth hadn't left my bedside unless it was to get me food
and water. Her friendship was keeping me anchored to the here
and now.

So many times I'd wished that the damn serum would finish
me off and let me climb off this wheel of torture, but it wasn't done
with me yet.

In between my turbulent fits I'd listened in on the conversations between my friends. The news that the GA had Felicity in
custody had lifted my spirits, but the disturbing fact that her father was still missing worried me, and the pack.

Sebastian had been good to his word and handed himself over to the GA. They extended him the courtesy of listening as he explained about Evermore and the serum. He'd exposed his vulnerabilities by telling them about his part in the death of my mother, and the blackmail threat Parker held over him. I was proud of my father, and I made a mental note to tell him that fact when I recovered.

'Morning.'

Elizabeth leaned forward and removed the flannel from my forehead and replaced it with a fresh one, the coolness giving me immediate relief from the burning beneath my skin.

I smiled at my friend. 'What time is it?'

'Ten past two. You've been drifting in and out of sleep for a few hours. Zak went back to the farm with Cody and the others to talk about what to do next.'

I licked my cracked lips and Elizabeth jumped up to grab a glass of water off the bedside table.

'Here, have a sip.'

She lifted me gently into a seated position and held the cup for me. The water tasted so good, and I drained the contents.

'Where's Sebastian?'

'He's back at Hood Academy talking to the GA. They want him to file a report against Parker and Felicity so they can take further action against them. He told me the GA are getting ready to leave as they're satisfied with the review.'

'They're leaving?'

'As far as I can tell. They've sided with Sebastian and there's some talk about reinstating him as headmaster when they go.'

'That's great news,' I said, flinching as a spasm of pain shot through my gut.

'Careful, Mia. You're still very weak.' She fluffed up my pillow and squeezed my hand as she sat beside me on the bed. 'Sebastian's honesty has saved him. They understand the strain he was under thanks to Parker's threat, and they're willing to give him another chance.'

I was happy, truly happy that Sebastian would be staying on at Hood Academy. It was more than a job to him; I understood that now. It was his ancestral home, and, I guess, mine too. I wasn't sure if that would even be a possibility now I was a fully fledged wolf, but I knew Sebastian wouldn't turn his back on me, wolf or not.

'What happens next?' I felt like I'd missed so much since I'd been here. The pack was still rallying around their alpha to eliminate the Evermore threat, Parker was out there somewhere doing God knows what, and I was stuck in bed drinking foul-smelling potions, and riding each wave of pain as it rushed through my system.

'Zak's liaising with the other alphas around the country to destroy the Evermore dispatch warehouses. Liam arrived the other day with a few of the lads from Somerset. They'd contacted Headmaster Gregory from the local academy and explained the situation. From what I hear the wolves and hunters worked together to take down the warehouse in Somerset, and I also heard that Adam rallied the Cornwall academy to approach the packs and tear down the Evermore branch in the south.'

'Did anyone tell Gregory about Ethan?' I hadn't dared bring up the subject of me killing the hunter until now. I could scarcely believe it myself. When I nearly killed Felicity in the woods, Elizabeth, Zak, and the rest of the pack hadn't been able to look at me let alone speak to me, and yet now I'd crossed that line.

'Zak explained Ethan's part in all this to him but he wasn't shocked. He said that Felicity was a regular visitor at the Somerset academy and the head was worried that our red-headed friend had been leading Ethan astray for some time.'

'That's the understatement of the year.'

Elizabeth giggled. 'He tricked us all, Mia. The bad guy turned good guy ruse had us all fooled.'

I shuffled then winced.

'You did what you had to do to survive, Mia. Anyone would have done the same in your situation.'

I smiled at my friend for her kind words but I knew that Ethan's death would haunt my dreams for a long while.

'Let's just be happy that Gregory is working with Zak on destroying Evermore,' she added. 'That news is something worth celebrating.'

She was right, of course. I was amazed at the news. Hunters and wolves working together was something I never thought I'd hear about, but it stirred something deep inside me. Sebastian had told me during our car journey that things were shifting. There was evidence of hunter-wolf relationships in my notebook. Blimey, even I was a living, breathing piece of that, but something else he'd said swam to the forefront of my mind. I'd been feverish at the time, but his conversation with Cody at my bedside was burnt into my memory. *I believe the barriers between the hunters and the wolves have been changing for some time, but clearly nobody dares talk about it. The horror of what Mr Parker has done might shine a light on a new era, Cody. One that you and Mia are already a part of.* Was it possible that we could create a new alliance between the werewolves and the hunters? Could we honour Dr Neale's legacy and stand by his oath to protect and serve? The thought excited me, and a new surge of power washed over me. For the first time in my life, I knew what I wanted to do, and I wasn't afraid to do it.

MY LEGS WERE still a bit shaky, but I was getting stronger every day. For the past week, Elizabeth had come with me each morning to the garden so we could work on our combat skills. Sebastian had taken a couple of wooden staffs from the academy, so we had weapons to train with.

'You keep dropping your left shoulder.' Miss Ross's voice was like a musical note as she wandered into the garden, and I rushed to hug her.

Elizabeth squealed at the sight of our friend and mentor.

'It's good to see you, girls,' she said lowering herself into the camping chair Sebastian kept handy should I need to rest. 'I'm glad you're getting better, Mia.'

'I still feel like vomiting over my own shoes every day, but Sebastian said that'll stop soon as the poison is nearly out of my system.'

'Glad to hear it!'

'What are you doing here?'

'Your brother told me you were up and about and I thought you might want some help with your training. I know how important it is to you that you stay in control.'

She wasn't wrong. Escaping a violent life changed something inside of me, and when I found that spark in my heart never to play the victim's role ever again, nothing would allow me to slip back into that darkness.

'May I?' She stood and walked across to Elizabeth, taking the staff out of her hand.

'I'll leave you guys to it then.' Elizabeth dashed off inside the cottage, and I made a mental note to yell at her later for abandoning me to the fate of a lethal hunter.

Shit. My lesson in recovery was about to start whether I was ready or not.

I'D FORGOTTEN HOW tough training with Miss Ross could be. I'd only had a few one-on-one sessions with her at Hood Academy before being integrated into main classes, and yet it seemed that now I was a werewolf Miss Ross wasn't going to give me any special treatment.

'How do you know so much about werewolf training?' I asked between gasps. 'I thought you only tutored the hunters.'

Miss Ross's smooth complexion hadn't even broken into a sweat as she'd parried and jabbed relentlessly at me for the past hour. She remained fresh while I looked like I'd been on a triathlon.

'I used to spar with your mother when she was a new wolf. We were only girls back then and didn't really understand the animosity between the packs and the hunters. Call it a naïve innocence.'

'You two were friends when you were teenagers then?' I'd known for a while that Miss Ross and my mum had been close friends, so close in fact that Miss Ross was also my godmother, but I didn't realise they'd been friends from such a young age.

'We were at school together,' she said, jabbing a fist at my head. I dodged and blocked her swing, which got me a satisfied grunt from my tutor. 'We were drawn together by some unknown force. Perhaps it was because we were so different from the other kids. We had an unspoken bond due to our heritage.'

'Did you fight with her?'

Miss Ross chuckled as she spun on her leg and knocked me to the ground with her foot. 'Oh yes! We used to train together like we're doing now. I helped her through her transition to a werewolf, and she helped me hone my skills as a tracker.'

I sat on the floor my chest heaving from the effort of breathing.

'She'd be very proud of you, Mia.'

She extended a hand to help me up, and I took it gratefully.

'Mum never wanted this for me though. She never wanted me to be a wolf.'

'Your mother didn't want either you or Zak to go through the turn. She wanted to protect her children from the pain, suffering, and mental torture of being a wolf. I think, despite the fact you did turn, she would be proud of how you handled yourself, how you coped with the transition, and the young woman you've become.'

'Thank you,' I whispered. It felt good to have someone recognise what I'd achieved. Not so long ago I'd wished that I could turn, longed for it because I thought it was the only way to feel like I belonged, and I'd been bitterly disappointed with my hybrid status. However, the more I read about my ancestors, the more I realised what a great honour it was to be different.

'Can I tell you a secret?'

One of Miss Ross's eyebrows rose as she waited for me to spill my news.

'Well, actually, I need to show you rather than tell you.'

This got her second eyebrow twitching high up on her forehead.

I took a deep breath and extended my arms out a little from my body. As I concentrated, the sharp claws stretched out from my fingers. I lifted my chin and opened my mouth enough to show the smooth curve of my fangs.

Miss Ross's eyes widened as she took in my hybrid frame. She approached and gently lifted my right hand, running her finger along the claw. Turning my hand over, she examined the points of my fingers where the claws replaced my fingernails. Her hands moved up to cup the sides of my face as she stared at my fangs and then right into my eyes. I saw something shimmering in her gaze, something I used to see in my mother's expression: joy, love, and pride.

'It's incredible, Mia, but how is it possible?'

I shook my hands, and the claws retracted along with my fangs. I'd only discovered this ability the other day when Elizabeth had left me alone to fetch a sandwich from the kitchen. Stretching out to grab a glass of water I'd watched my claws shoot out. It had stunned me at first, but also fascinated me. I'd been able to retract and extend them at will for several minutes until Lizzie arrived back. I hadn't told her. I don't know why, but in a way, I was glad that Miss Ross was the first to know.

'I think me hearing that Parker was responsible for my mother's death triggered my turn because I was so angry. I'd never felt rage like it before. I'm not sure, but I think I'm always going to be a hybrid with the ability to turn only if I need to.'

'The full moon is in two days. If you're a true wolf, then you won't be able to resist the turn. It's the law of nature.'

I nodded as I remembered her lesson on full moon activity. 'Are you going to tell Zak?'

I shook my head. Zak had been sensitive to the point of annoying recently. I knew he was worried about me, but I needed him to appreciate how tough I could be. Cody knew how resilient I could be. He had been helping me control my senses as I lay in bed recovering. He understood that my differences were what made me unique.

'No, he'll only worry even more about me. By the time the full moon rises in the sky, I'll be ready to join the pack at the farm. I'll deal with whatever happens when it happens.'

'Probably a wise decision. Your brother still thinks of you as his little sister, and I doubt that'll ever change.'

Our exchange was interrupted as Sebastian strode out of the back door, lifting his hand in a little wave when he spotted his fellow tutor.

'Miss Ross, how good to see you.'

She nodded her head but took a small step backward. Evidently, the breach in their friendship hadn't been healed after my father's craziness, and Sebastian remained at arm's length.

'The GA has left,' he said, either ignoring or not noticing Miss Ross's standoffish manner. 'They packed up this morning and handed the academy back to me.'

He was beaming, and I felt a tug of pride for him. Without Parker's blackmail threat, and with the destruction of Evermore, he was free to run the academy as a headmaster should. Of course, I had wondered what his intentions were in that direction but hadn't been sure how to broach the subject. As it was, I needn't have worried as Miss Ross had it covered.

'Do you intend to train those girls to kill and torture the werewolf community?'

'Absolutely not. There are going to be a lot of changes in the future, Miss Ross, and I hope you'll join me in implementing them.'

'What kind of changes?'

'For one, I've rewritten the hunters' oath.'

I gasped and covered my mouth with my hand. He wasn't kidding when he said big changes. That oath was first recorded in 1862, and now Sebastian was going to rip apart a piece of history.

'Is that wise?' I asked.

'You haven't heard it yet.' He was grinning like an excited schoolboy, and I couldn't help but get swept up in his euphoria.

'Go on then, Sebastian,' Miss Ross said, crossing her arms across her chest. 'Share it with us.'

He cleared his throat, and I stuffed down the urge to giggle.

'To every pack, a cub is born, and every hunter gets their dawn. Nurturing friendships that grow deeper, united together as an Oath Keeper.'

The forest seemed to hold its breath along with Miss Ross and me. It was beautiful. Right there in the heart of the forest, surrounded by the wonder of nature I felt a lightness in my chest. With a few simple changes, Sebastian had forever changed the course of history for the hunters.

'I don't know what to say,' Miss Ross whispered, clearly as much in awe as I was. 'You've done a wonderful thing, Sebastian.'

He huffed and rolled his shoulders back.

'But will the GA accept this?' she added. 'They've stood by the original oath for hundreds of years, what makes you think they'll conform to this?'

He glanced over at me and smiled. 'I shared something else with the GA when I was questioned. Something that I hadn't told them before. They knew I was a hunter, but they'd never traced my bloodline. When I told them I was a direct descendant of Dr Neale they came round to my way of thinking.'

'You're a descendant of the first hunter?' Miss Ross's jaw dropped at his revelation, but then her face changed as she calculated the rest. 'Oh, Mia. That means you were his—'

I held up a hand to stop her. 'Yep, great-great-great whatever! I know, it's cool.'

'Well, if the GA is happy then I'm happy,' she said, offering her hand to Sebastian.

He took it with good grace and beamed at my godmother.

'There's something else. They want me to join the GA as chief consultant. I'll still be based from Hood Academy, but all GA policies will go through me.'

'That's amazing!' I cried, genuinely pleased for him.

'It means I need to find a new headmaster for Hood Academy, or perhaps a headmistress. What do you think?' Sebastian asked Miss Ross.

I'd never seen her so gobsmacked in the short time I'd known her. It was a huge position but an honour to receive. Taking control of the academy and the future of the hunter line was an incredible task, one that I knew, as did my father, Miss Ross was fully capable of handling.

'Yes,' she said softly. 'I'd be delighted to accept.'

I couldn't stop myself from squealing as I leaped at Miss Ross to wrap her in a tight hug. Times were changing, and everything was going to be different from now on.

FOURTEEN

Sitting at my bedroom window, back at the Mills family farm, I gazed up at the darkening sky. It wouldn't be long until nightfall and the rise of the full moon. Cody had said he'd stay with me for the turn, but I'd brushed him off saying I'd done it once in front of an audience and I quite fancied the next time being a private affair. He understood and went to join the pack for whatever ritual they had on such a night.

The truth was I wasn't sure if I would turn. I suspected that I was back to being a hybrid and only something truly horrific would trigger my inner werewolf.

I'd eventually told Elizabeth my suspicions and hoped she'd help me deal with whatever happened over the next few hours.

'Hey, Mia.' Ari burst through my bedroom door and bounded up to my side followed by Lizzie. 'Aren't you coming down to join the pack?'

I circled the little wolf into a tight hug and pulled her up onto my lap. She had proved herself to be an incredibly capable young girl, leading the other pack kids to safety and keeping them calm. Her parents were bursting with pride and Ari's mother had taken to trailing after her making sure everyone she spoke with knew about her darling daughter. It was cute.

'Not this time, Ari. I wanted to do this privately, you know, until I get the hang of it.'

Ari giggled and pulled on her pigtail. 'I know what you mean. I threw up in front of Ben Clifton when I turned, and he teased me for weeks after.'

'Oh really, is Ben your boyfriend then?'

'Ugh, no way. He's a smelly boy that lives next door.'

Elizabeth laughed out loud at Ari's reaction, and I couldn't help but giggle at her disgusted expression. She was only ten years old and had plenty of time to learn about boys, crushes, and falling in love.

There was a light tap on the door, and Ari's mum stuck her head through the gap.

'Sorry to interrupt but Ari needs to head downstairs, the alpha is addressing the pack in a few minutes.'

Ari leaped from my lap and hurtled out of the room, then thundered down the stairs. I had a sneaking suspicion that the little wolf didn't like young Ben Clifton because she had a crush on my brother.

'Are you okay, Mrs Fletcher?'

The petite lady smiled and walked into the centre of the room. She fiddled with her sleeve as her gaze wandered over the furniture, walls, and my belongings. She couldn't stop fidgeting, and it was making my head spin. I stood up and grasped her hands in my own.

'Are you okay?' I repeated.

'I spoke with Dr Roberts about Ari and Toni, her sister.' Her voice grew quiet as she brought forward the memory of her lost daughter. 'He was interested in testing Ari's blood to see why she had survived that nasty stuff that Evermore was peddling.'

'Did he find anything?'

Her eyes filled with tears and the tiny woman let out a loud sob before collapsing onto the end of my bed. Elizabeth rushed to close the door, and I dropped to my knees in front of her, patting her hands and offering soothing sounds.

'He told me his suspicions as to why some of the children survived, and I was so ashamed.'

I peeked at Lizzie over the top of Mrs Fletcher's head, and she shrugged. No, Sebastian hadn't told me about his suspicions either. I was almost too afraid to ask.

'What suspicions does he have?'

Mrs Fletcher raised her tear-stained face and peered at me, holding my gaze and tensing her jaw.

'Ari is only half wolf. You see, I had an affair and only discovered I was pregnant after we split up. Pete never knew that Ari wasn't his.'

I was amazed that she'd shared such a sensitive secret with us, but the cogs were turning in my mind as I processed what she was saying and compared it with what Sebastian had said.

'Can I ask you a question? Did you have an affair with a hunter?'

More sobbing and shaking and plenty of tears but eventually Mrs Fletcher nodded.

'Yes, he was a hunter, and I was a wolf. My pack would have killed me if they'd discovered our relationship. I couldn't talk to anyone, and I prayed that when she reached sixteen, she would turn like her dad and me.'

It all clicked into place. The serum had killed her sister but only forced Ari to turn. That same serum had caused me to have hallucinations, sickness, and pain but I'd ultimately remained the same.

'Have you seen Ari turn?'

'Yes, we watched it happen over and over.'

'What are you thinking, Mia?' Elizabeth had seen that look on my face before.

'Ari is half wolf and half hunter. She's a hybrid, like me.'

Mrs Fletcher's eyes grew wide. 'Does that mean she can stop the turn?'

'Maybe,' I said. 'If it's okay with you, Ari could stay with me tonight instead of joining the rest of the pack. I'll see if it's possible for us to stay human on a full moon.'

'Oh, Mia, that would be wonderful. Thank you, thank you so much.'

'It does mean that Ari should know the truth about her dad, Mrs Fletcher,' I said gently. Telling your daughter that her dad isn't really her dad would be tough and yet ironically, I couldn't help but notice how the little wolf's life mirrored my own in that respect.

'I know,' she said. 'I'll tell her.'

She rushed out of the room in search of her daughter. I was pretty sure Ari wouldn't thank me for taking her away from Zak's big speech, but if I was right, there was a strong possibility that the two of us could resist the full moon.

'Will you stay with us, Lizzie?'

My friend walked over and sat beside me on the bed taking my hand in hers and squeezing my fingers.

'I'm not going anywhere. No matter what happens I'll stay beside you and Ari until morning.'

THE HOWLS OF the wolves started as soon as the moon reached its apex. I kept the lights off in my bedroom so no one could see us from the woods. Ari and I stood holding hands in the middle of the room, sweat pouring down both of our faces. Lizzie waited by the door, ready to escape if we did turn and Ari's youth and inability to control her actions caused her to attack our friend.

My skin tingled like I was connected to a mild electrical current, but it wasn't uncomfortable. I could feel the same tremors running through Ari's fingers and felt immense respect for the youngster who had paid careful attention to my instructions.

Not once did she moan, question, or argue with me. When Mrs Fletcher dropped her off at my room, Ari's eyes were puffy but she seemed okay with herself. It wasn't my place to get involved in their family discussions, but I'd wanted the little wolf to know she had a friend if she needed one.

'I'm okay, Mia,' she said once her mother had left. 'Daddy is still my daddy.'

I was overwhelmed with love and loyalty for this youngster who was one of the strongest people I'd had the honour to meet.

She happily listened to my story of the hybrid ancestry and the information I'd found in Dr Neale's notebook and this helped her to piece it together with her mother's revelation.

Mrs Fletcher joined her husband, Zak, Cody, and the rest of the pack in the woods, telling them that Ari felt a responsibility to look after her friend Mia. They all thought it was cute that the little wolf was looking after the newbie and they left us to it.

As we both fought the power of the moon, I believed that statement was partly true. We fought it together, hand in hand. The little hybrid wolf and her hybrid mentor. I hoped that this worked and we both stayed human. There was going to be a tough road ahead for the Fletcher family as the truth would inevitably come out now, but if Ari was saved the horrific pain of turning every four weeks, then it was worth it.

Miss Ross entered the room, and I heard her whispered exchange with Elizabeth.

'That's it, they've all turned and are in the woods. The moon's at its peak.'

'What do we do now?'

'We wait and see if they can hold on a little while longer.'

I squeezed Ari's fingers a bit tighter and smiled down into her beautiful, shining face. There was a determination in her eyes, and I could feel her power shuddering through our connection.

My limbs were visibly trembling now but the pain I'd experienced at Hood Academy that night hadn't manifested. Tremors, the sweats, and a thumping headache were all that plagued me at that moment.

Like a wave washing over the pair of us our pulses slowed down, our heart rate settled, and we dropped to sit on the floor together, exhausted.

'We did it,' Ari whispered, her clammy face illuminated in the light of the moon shining through the window.

'We did,' I agreed, circling my arm around the little hybrid. 'I'm so proud of you.'

'Well done, girls.' Miss Ross sat next to us as the moonlight bathed us in its glow. 'You've achieved the impossible tonight, and I think this is going to help many of the children who survived the serum.'

'Surely not *all* of their parents were unfaithful,' Elizabeth said, joining us on the floor.

'No, the DNA has travelled through generations. It might be that many years ago a hunter and wolf married in secret and brought children into the world and their descendants eventually wound up back in segregated communities believing that wolves and hunters shouldn't mix.'

'The hunter gene would remain in their DNA even if they married another hunter and had a baby. There's every possibility that two hunters could have a hybrid baby without ever knowing.'

'A lot of children survived the serum.'

'It's a good thing, Lizzie. With that evidence and Sebastian's new oath we've got a chance of living in harmony.'

We all sat in silence for a few moments taking in the enormity of the situation. History was being made, and we were key players. It felt good.

The companionable quiet was shattered by the sound of gunfire in the woods. We jumped to our feet, and I ran to the window, looking out at the forest bathed in the eerie glow of the moon.

More shots were fired followed by a keening sound that filled me with dread. Howls carried on the breeze, and I tried to distinguish between the sounds. Would I recognise Zak's cry if I wasn't in my wolf form?

'What the hell's happening?' Elizabeth grabbed her wooden staff and headed for the door before I'd even pulled on my shoes.

'I'm not sure, but it doesn't sound good.'

Another shot, another wail. My gut rolled, and I fought the nausea that threatened to overwhelm me.

'Ari, I need you to stay here. Lock the kitchen door behind us and don't come out no matter what you hear.' I grabbed the girl's shoulders and held her tightly. 'We're going to go help the pack, but I need someone here to look after anyone who makes it back home.

She puffed out her chest and tapped her forehead with her tiny hand. 'Aye, aye, Captain.'

We left her behind, her small face the last thing I saw before she slammed the door and the bolt slid home. She was safe at least. Now we had to find her family and make sure they were safe too.

'We stick together until we work out what we're up against,' Miss Ross said, her authoritarian teacher's voice calm and steady.

As one we melted into the forest unsure of what we might find but ready to take on any danger that faced us.

FIFTEEN

Nothing could have prepared any of us for what we found as we moved deeper into the forest. Elizabeth fell over the first body, and I found the second. No longer in their wolf form, the two pack members lay sprawled across the floor, their naked bodies smeared with blood and grime.

Lizzie threw up behind a holly bush, but by some miracle I kept control of the bile rising up my throat.

'Are they dead?' Elizabeth's voice was barely audible.

'Yes.' Miss Ross felt for the pulse in their neck. 'There's nothing we can do for them. We can return later to recover their bodies, but for now we need to press on.'

More shots echoed through the trees, further ahead of us nearer to the academy.

'Have the GA changed their mind and come back to finish off the pack?' It was the only logical explanation I could come up with.

'The GA doesn't use guns. A hunter uses natural weapons to defend themselves, like the wooden staff. This is something else.'

By the gleam in Miss Ross's eye, I believed she had her own thoughts on who, or what, we were about to find but I wasn't sure I wanted to know in advance.

A series of snarls and cries to our immediate left had us running in that direction. We burst through the trees to find a small brown wolf pinned down by two students, one holding a gun in shaky hands and the other a small crossbow. Shock reverberated through me at the sight.

Hood Academy students, kitted out in their grey school jumpsuits, were attacking the wolves in the forest at gunpoint. My mind tried to make sense of it, but before I could fathom an answer, Miss Ross had struck the nearest girl with the butt of her staff and was rounding on the other.

'Who sent you here tonight?' she snapped, circling the girl.

'The headmaster,' she said, her voice shaking almost as much as her hand. 'He said we were under attack, rounded us all up, and gave us a weapon. I've never killed anyone...anything before.'

The brown wolf hadn't run away, and I realised it had a bullet wound in its back leg.

With Miss Ross dealing with the student it gave me time to tend to the wolf. I dragged my scarf from my neck and wrapped it around the leg. Before my eyes, the wolf disappeared, and Mrs Fletcher lay before me. I'd never seen the wolves return to their human form before and I had been in no fit state to remember my own return. It was like the fur melted away exposing broken bones which shifted back into position as one.

Ari's mum moaned as she collapsed to the forest floor.

'Oh my God.' The student dropped to her knees, throwing the gun away to the side in disgust. Elizabeth scooped it up and slid it into her waistband.

'The headmaster you're talking about, is he called Sebastian?' Miss Ross continued her interrogation.

'No, the head is Mr Parker. He's been head for a few months now.'

I sat back on my heels and stared at Miss Ross, a message passing between us. The girls didn't know Parker was no longer head.

Parker had armed the students and sent them into the woods even though most of them weren't fully trained. He'd used young girls as a weapon and didn't care if they were slaughtered in the process. We'd found dead wolves, but I was under no misconception that somewhere in these woods we'd find dead students too, young girls who faced the wrong wolves and never lived long enough to see the yellow of their eyes.

'Go, find Zak and the others,' said Miss Ross. 'I'll take this girl with me, and we'll help Mrs Fletcher. It's probably nearer to the academy than the farm so I'll get her to the hospital wing. If you find any more wounded send them there.'

I nodded and left Mrs Fletcher moaning on the ground. Elizabeth joined me as we sprinted off into the night.

We found other pack members wandering the woods, dazed at the sudden attack. Fortunately, my scent was familiar to all of them, and I was able to guide them in the direction of home or the school and Miss Ross.

'I wish we could find Zak and Cody,' I said pushing the branches out of my way.

'I know. There haven't been any shots for a while. Do you think the wolves have killed all the students?'

'God, I hope not. Parker's used them to try and start a war, and it's up to us to make sure that he doesn't manage it.'

'How the hell are we supposed to stop him, Mia? The man's dangerous. He's prepared to sacrifice teenagers.'

I couldn't answer her. I had no idea how to stop someone like Parker. I'd spent so long fighting his daughter that the prospect of coming face to face with her dad never dawned on me. I knew that he probably wasn't in these woods though; he wouldn't want to get his hands dirty. I shivered as I remem-

161

bered his conversation with Felicity about framing Sebastian for everything. Parker had turned getting away with murder into an art form.

The trees ahead rustled and we both braced ourselves ready to fight. Together we gasped as Terry staggered into view, his naked body covered in blood. Elizabeth shrugged off her coat and wrapped it around his waist, nestling herself in the crook of his arm to help support him. He'd been shot before, but it was a clean wound and healed quickly thanks to his werewolf healing abilities. This was an altogether different situation.

From this angle I could see two bullet wounds, both in his leg; he had a crossbow bolt sticking out from his shoulder and another in his abdomen. He coughed, and a cloud of blood spurted across the floor.

Pitching to his knees, he crumpled to the ground taking Elizabeth with him.

'Where's Zak?' Panic laced my voice as I watched my friend bleed all over the earth. 'Where's my brother?'

'We got separated,' he wheezed. 'Near the school.'

He was spent, that small piece of information enough to wear him out beyond exhaustion. Blood poured down his chest from the injured shoulder and mingled with the fresh blood seeping from the hole in his gut.

'I don't know what to do,' I said to no one in particular.

'Look for Zak. I'll try and get Terry to the school. Miss Ross will patch him up. He's tough, Mia, don't worry.'

I nodded at my friend and taking one last look at Terry I shot off into the trees.

The forest was silent, not even the nocturnal animals dared to move. The moon had begun its descent but still lit up the area like the floodlights on a football field.

I was close to the school now and crept silently to the edge of the treeline to see if I could spot Parker or the wolves. Soft cries filled the air, and I felt a tug on my heartstrings

SHELLEY WILSON

as I saw the huddles of young girls clinging to one another. They hadn't asked to be put in this position. They'd arrived at school ready to start their training in the safe environment of the academy building. At no point were they expecting to be sent out into the woods during a full moon armed with guns and told to kill on sight.

Should I speak to them? Could I convince them that Parker wasn't the headmaster anymore and they didn't have to follow his orders? I doubted they would believe me after everything that had happened. It was common knowledge that Mia Roberts had followed the pack and rejected the oath. If only they knew about the changes Sebastian would make.

My skin crawled as Parker emerged from the back of the school building, Felicity at his side. How the hell did he get her away from the GA? That didn't matter now. I had the two of them together in one place, and all I needed to do was find a way to stop them.

I watched Parker move around the girls appraising them with predatory eyes as I contemplated various ridiculous acts of bravery. He flicked at something on his jacket, dusting the sleeve and rubbing his blackened hands on a handkerchief from his pocket. I didn't want to think about the stains on his hands or the blackish smudge that now coated the cloth. No doubt he'd tortured some unfortunate soul. His stance reeked of authority as if he'd already won when I knew he'd lost everything. Perhaps this was his plan all along; return to the scene of the crime and kill everyone in a blaze of glory.

Blimey, I needed to stop watching Cody's action films.

I surveyed the students. They clung together wearing matching jumpsuits and school regulation pumps, but that was all. A large crate of guns lay open on the lawn a few feet away from them but they eyed it nervously. I couldn't see a weapon of any kind on their person apart from the wooden staff Felicity was twirling. Even Parker appeared unarmed.

He really believed he was safe. Safe from attack, safe from discovery. This was my chance. Taking a deep breath, I stood up, strolled out of the treeline, and headed across the lawn towards the assembled group.

Felicity was the first to spot me and screamed with fury. She sprinted to meet me, but her father grabbed at her arm stopping her in her tracks.

'No need, pumpkin, she'll be dead soon enough.'

I came to a stop a few feet away and held my arms out to the side readying myself to release my claws. I didn't want to freak the students out, so if I could keep them hidden for as long as possible it would be for the best. It was tough to ignore the itch just beneath my skin as I watched Parker and his red-headed daughter snarl at me.

'You're a tiresome creature, Miss Roberts,' Parker barked across the lawn. 'You've managed to unravel my carefully crafted plans and bring about the destruction of my entire business empire. If I didn't have to kill you, I'd be of a mind to offer you a job. You've got a certain way with manipulation that I admire.'

'I'm flattered. First I beat your daughter at the assessments, then I impress you with my handiwork. Perhaps I'm the daughter you wish you'd had.'

Parker was way ahead of me and kept a tight grip on Felicity's arm. Goading her was a cheap trick, but it felt great. Divide and conquer them was my only plan.

'Perhaps you should have left her to the GA where she couldn't show you up.'

Felicity's face matched her hair colour as she tugged at her father's grip, but Mr Parker held firm.

'The GA are a bunch of fools, my dear, and can't see the corruption in their ranks. Did you know there are a dozen GA agents loyal to me? No, I don't suppose you would.'

That explained the kidnappings. The children from the lab had spoken about men in black taking them from their homes. Parker clearly hadn't heard about Sebastian's reinstatement or his new role at the GA. I smiled to myself as I thought about Parker's men getting their comeuppance.

'Do you find something funny, Miss Roberts?'

'You've broken Felicity out of the GA using their own men. Don't you think someone will notice and come looking for you both?'

'Oh, I think the GA will have enough to deal with clearing up all the dead vermin from the woods.'

I flinched. He wanted the wolves dead. All of them. I had to stop him.

'You don't belong here anymore,' I said, loud enough for the gathered students to hear me. 'The GA dismissed you, arrested *her*, and reinstated Sebastian as head of the academy. What you're forcing these girls to do is against the oath.'

Murmured whispers rippled through the assembled students.

'That's right,' I shouted. 'You've all broken the hunters' oath and could be punished. If I were you, I'd make your way back to your dormitories and wait for Dr Roberts.'

'Stay where you are!' Parker snapped. His words echoed through the night air and startled the group who began crying again.

I needed to get the girls to safety before engaging with Felicity and her father. I had no idea if Parker could fight. I'd never seen him in action even though he was a hunter. I'd seen him intimidate, bully, and embarrass, but I'd never seen him swing a staff.

The low howl of a wolf in the distance followed by the response of others answered my prayers. Zak's call. I did recognise it after all. I breathed a sigh of relief on hearing the sound. He was calling the pack, and that could only mean he was rounding them up for an attack. As he wasn't too close, I could only assume he'd found more students in the woods.

The sound briefly distracted Parker and his daughter, and without giving it too much thought, I burst into a run and barrelled straight into Felicity knocking her to the ground. Parker snatched at me grazing my arm with his fingertips but missing out on a firm grip. I kept running until I reached the girls, who shuffled backward in fright and surprise.

'Run, all of you!' I shouted. 'Get to the hospital wing and find Miss Ross. She'll tell you what to do. Go!'

They didn't need much persuasion as they sprinted off across the lawn towards the school building. The howls in the woods grew louder. Zak was heading this way.

'You stupid bitch.' Felicity jumped at me, punching me square in the face. I staggered backward almost losing my footing. I could feel the blood dripping down my face, but within seconds I felt my claws snap into place and my fangs appear.

I swiped at my nemesis catching the top of her arm. She yelped and jumped clear. The sound of approaching wolves filled my head, the soft boom of their paws on the compacted earth, their breath a faint whisper on the wind.

I only needed to stall these two long enough for the alpha to arrive.

Felicity thrust her staff forward but I blocked it with ease. I was getting better and faster at anticipating her moves.

'I'm going to kill you for what you did to Ethan,' she hissed.

'He'd still be alive today if you hadn't involved him.' I knew it was a low blow to turn Ethan's death on her and from the flash of anger in her eyes I'd hit a nerve.

She snarled, and I almost laughed. If she wanted to know what a real snarl was like I was only too happy to show her.

I filled my lungs and roared, releasing my full hybrid power. The startled expression on Felicity's face was worth it. I reached back ready to strike another blow when Parker assaulted me from the side. He wielded a long cane like something out of a Sherlock Holmes movie with a heavy brass ball on the end. My teeth shuddered as it connected with my head. Stars danced across my vision as I tried to keep Felicity in my view. They were tag teaming me now, circling me like vultures around a fresh kill.

The cane landed on my shoulder blade, and I heard the loud crack as it fractured. Pain seared through me as I howled. Felicity flicked her staff up, catching my chin and sending me sprawling onto the ground. Parker stood over me his cane poised, ready to bring it down onto my skull. I tried to lift myself up but the pain shot through my arm and I slid back to the floor. Parker's eyes clouded over as he lifted his cane.

'Time to die, Miss Roberts.'

I waited for the blow, but it never came; a blur of fur and fangs filled my vision as a huge brown wolf hooked its teeth into Parker and dragged him away, his screams filling the empty space he'd left behind.

Felicity became hysterical, whirling her staff in all directions trying to cause damage but not hitting anything in the process. The gurgled sounds of her father's demise distracted her. She screamed her fury and threw the staff at a golden wolf who guarded me where I lay, but the wood fell harmlessly under the claws of the pack. Wolves swarmed the grounds, and I caught the scent of everyone I knew and loved.

Surrounded, Felicity still refused to give in. She lashed out at anything that came too close to her as she crept closer to her father's body. Parker's lifeless eyes stared into the star-filled sky, blood soaked the front of his shirt, and his torn throat glistened under the moonlight. I tried to push down the need to vomit. Sobbing and shaking, Felicity knelt over her father and the wolves seemed to hold their position as if giving her that split second to grieve.

That split second was all she needed to unhook the gun from Parker's belt, the gun I hadn't spotted before, and wave it at the wolves. She settled the barrel on Zak, and I saw her finger twitch as she squeezed.

The gunshot made me scream, the sound too loud for me to deal with. I struggled to my knees, my eyes darting all over for Zak, but he remained where he had been, as strong and powerful as ever. My brain couldn't work it out until I spotted Sebastian, his arm outstretched with a smoking gun in his hand.

Felicity was on the floor, blood pouring from a wound to her shoulder. She screamed and swore, and for a brief moment, I was relieved to hear it. He hadn't killed her, but Sebastian had stopped her from killing my brother.

SIXTEEN

Miss Ross was in full control when we arrived at the hospital wing of Hood Academy. Students and pack members sat together, helping each other. My heart swelled with pride at the sight.

Cody helped me through the main door where the young girl we'd met in the woods greeted me. Her face was tear-stained and her eyes ringed with bruises from crying, but she looked like she'd pulled herself together.

'I'm Jenny,' she said stretching out her hand and helping me into a nearby seat. 'I wanted to thank you for not killing me earlier.'

I huffed and instantly recognised the family trait.

'Mia,' I said with a wave of my hand. 'I never had any intention of killing you. I only wanted to stop Parker from starting a war between the hunters and the wolves.'

'I know, Miss Ross filled me in on everything on the way back here. She's a wonderful tutor. I hope she stays.'

'Oh, don't you worry about that. Miss Ross will be around for a long time.'

'Do you need anything? Bandages, pain relief, water?'

'No, thanks, I've got it covered.' I knew that my bones were already healing and knitting back together as I could feel it like a burning sensation beneath my skin. 'How's Terry? Did Elizabeth make it here okay?'

Jenny shook her head. 'I haven't seen anyone called Terry, and if Elizabeth is the blonde girl you were with in the woods, then she hasn't been here either.'

Panic bubbled up in my chest. Terry was in a bad way and needed help. Yes, he would heal eventually but not if there were bullets lodged in his body or crossbow bolts still wedged in his side.

Cody scanned the assembled group but finally he glanced at me and shook his head.

'We've got to find them,' I said to him.

'I know. We'll head back out into the woods, and hopefully we can pick up their scent.'

Jenny left us at the door as we hurried out into the car park. Zak was still in his wolf form refusing to return to being human in case he needed to protect his pack from further attack, which was fortunate for us.

His immense head swivelled in our direction as we tore across the gravel car park. The other pack members who stood with him melted away to give us privacy.

'Terry was hurt, badly, and hasn't made it to the hospital wing. I think him and Lizzie are still out there somewhere.'

Zak bobbed his head to let me know he understood and then lifted his head to howl into the sky. From within the trees, I heard the returning cries of the wolves still patrolling the area. My brother approached and nudged my elbow with his large snout, pushing me towards the forest. He wanted me to run with him, brother and sister.

I stared up at the full moon still visible in the sky. I'd passed my own test to see if a hybrid could control its shift, but now I was about to see if a hybrid could turn when the need arose.

SHELLEY WILSON

Cody's warm fingers intertwined with mine and I gazed up into his sparkling blue eyes.

'Together,' he whispered.

I leaned in and kissed him.

'Together,' I agreed.

Taking a deep breath I concentrated on my body, feeling for the bones and muscles, picturing the tendons and ligaments that joined it all together, and then the heat washed over me like an explosion. The pain was instant as my bones began to break and my skin rippled.

I was aware that some Hood Academy students were standing outside the nurse's office door watching as Cody and I turned, but I didn't mind. I was proud of who I was, and I wanted everyone to know it.

WE RAN THROUGH the woods as one pack, sniffing out injured wolves and startling any stray students. Zak ordered some to stay behind and help guide everyone home. As we ripped up the earth with our paws, we found pockets of hunters and wolves huddled together.

Ari's father stood as we entered the clearing where he and another pack member sat with a young girl from the academy. The two men were draped in blankets but were unharmed.

'I heard your cry, but I didn't want to scare the young lass by returning to my wolf form,' he told us. I could understand his words perfectly even though it was his scent I recognised rather than his physical looks. 'I saw young Elizabeth with Terry. They were heading back to the Mills Farm. He didn't look good, but the lass was looking after him well.'

A deep rumble erupted from the back of Zak's throat causing the student to flinch and shy away from the wolves surrounding her.

'I will,' Mr Fletcher said in response to Zak's request. 'We'll take her back to the academy straight away.'

It was a relief to hear that Lizzie and Terry were making their way to the farm. I knew Terry was injured, and they were both probably shattered from the exertion of manoeuvring through the woods, but if they made it to the farm I knew someone would be there to tend to Terry's wounds.

I hoped Ari was okay too. The young wolf had been left alone and in charge of the farmhouse. I knew she could handle it, but I hoped hearing the cries from the woods hadn't worried her too much. Strong or not, she was still only a little girl.

We left Mr Fletcher and adjusted our route to take us back home. I was eager to see Elizabeth and check she was okay.

Running through the woods, I marvelled at the sensation of my powerful frame. Long ago I'd run through these same woods as a tearful teenager hiding from my problems. I'd come such a long way, and now I was free. That freedom felt incredible as the wind tore through my fur and my paws pounded the fallen leaves. The moon illuminated everything that was beautiful about the forest. The colours that changed with the shadows, the textures of the moss and bark, and the crunch of the leaves as the seasons turned. I'd never felt more alive.

Zak and Cody growled at the same time, and it took me a few seconds to sense the problem. The stars in the sky disappeared behind a haze, and the scents of the forest changed, becoming harsh and toxic. Something was burning.

My eyes caught sight of the flames above the treetops in the distance, and my stomach knotted. There was only one thing that would burn so fiercely out here, and that was the Mills farmhouse.

Panic clenched my insides as I understood the connection. Parker had been dusting ash off his coat and wiping soot from his hands when I saw him on the lawn. He had found the house, discovered where the wolves lived, and destroyed it. We had brought Ethan here and in our naivety we'd trusted that he'd keep the location a secret. His deceit ran deeper than we had realised and suddenly I wasn't so upset that I'd ripped his throat out.

The wolves darted in all directions unable to comprehend what was happening. I broke through the trees into the back garden of the house and came to an abrupt stop. Flames engulfed the entire building, licking up the sides of the walls, and blistering the paint on the wooden window frames. Smoke poured out of the kitchen door, which stood wide open. A sob caught in my throat and came out as a growl. The flames fanned out, leaving nothing untouched.

A strangled cry bubbled up from my throat, and I realised I was back in my human form. I hadn't even felt the shift or registered any pain. Looking around me I saw only wolves, all of them staring at the house, the flames dancing in the reflection of their eyes. I snatched a pair of joggers and T-shirt off the washing line and hurried to dress.

There was no way I could get close to the house; the flames were too fierce. Crumpling to the ground, I broke down. Ari, Elizabeth, and Terry were in there. Had they realised what was happening? Were they trapped? Or did the smoke kill them before the flames? Even after his death, Parker was still able to inflict pain and misery.

I tilted my head back and screamed into the night.

A soft shout caught my attention as if someone had heard my screams and was answering from the heavens. I opened my eyes and looked around. The wolves moved off as one towards the back of the house, and I scrambled to my bare feet and followed.

The white picket fence was blistering from the heat of the fire as we trailed around the edge of the property. Zak led the way, his deep brown fur glistening in the firelight. There was movement up ahead, and as the thick smoke parted briefly, I saw a blonde head of hair shining like a beacon.

'Lizzie!' I shouted as I launched into a sprint, barging past the wolves who stood between my friend and me.

She barrelled her way towards me, and we flew into each other's arms. Her hair smelt of smoke and her face was covered in soot and grime, but she was very much alive.

'This way, come quickly.' She herded me to the side and urged the wolves to follow. We headed for the garage adjacent to the farm, still untouched by the flames that decimated the farmhouse.

'Mia! You're here.' Ari shot out of the doorway, and I dropped to my knees to hug the little wolf. Relief flooded through me, and I sobbed once more.

One by one the wolves' masks dissolved until everyone was in their human form. Blankets and random pieces of clothing were distributed from the laundry that backed onto the garage block. Elizabeth tugged me through the door and there, lying on the flatbed of the Mills family truck, was Terry, languishing among the sacks of potatoes, his wolfish grin shining out from his sooty face.

'I don't know about being a wolf, you should be a bloody cat with all those lives you have.' I leaned across the side of the truck to kiss Terry's cheek.

He laughed out loud, and the sound melted something in my chest. I had thought they were gone, all of them, and for the briefest of moments, I was utterly broken.

Cody snaked his arm around my waist and slapped his brother on the shoulder, which made him wince, and all of us laugh. Zak stood on the other side of the truck and smiled at his friend, the relief clear on his face as much as on my own. Ari swung herself up onto the truck and nestled in next to Terry, a beaming smile on her beautiful young face.

I glanced around me as if seeing my friends and family for the first time. We were all hot and sweaty, covered in twigs, soot, and blood, and wearing mismatched clothing, but we were together. This was my pack, and I would follow them to the ends of the earth.

SEVENTEEN

The car pulled through the tall, wrought-iron gates and into the winding driveway of Hood Academy. It seemed a lifetime ago that Sebastian first brought me here as a new student.

The massive wooden doors of the school stood open as we pulled up outside and I saw the throng of people congregating in the entrance hall. Miss Ross stood on the top step greeting everyone as they arrived and I had to smile at her choice of wardrobe.

'I thought headmistresses had to wear stuffy suits and billowing cloaks,' I teased as I joined her.

'Then you're at the wrong school.' She winked, her bright blue tracksuit perfectly complementing her dark skin and reflecting in the twinkle of her eye.

I left her shaking hands with another group of students and wandered inside to see what other changes the new headmistress had made. At first glance everything looked the same. The comfortable sofas, the wood panelling, and the chandeliers were still there, but there was a new sign on the glazed office door. Miss Ross was in charge of Hood Academy now, and the wording on the plaque told everyone that fact. To the right of the head's office had been the small store cupboard, which housed the secret entrance to the basement laboratories. The cupboard was gone now, and with a bit of remodelling the space had been developed into a respectable entrance to the science labs.

It had been Sebastian's idea to continue working on natural remedies that could help both wolf and hunter. He'd abandoned his cure for lycanthropy and had instead begun to work on salves for dressing wounds, tonics for fever, and a serum to reduce the pain of turning at the full moon. The GA had agreed to fund the venture and were hoping it would create a pioneering science-based diploma for future students.

The excited chatter of the girls who came and went down the stairs to the labs told me the corridor of rooms, which had housed such barbaric activities below, had also received a remodel.

'Mia!' I spun around to see Elizabeth and Adam making their way through the masses of students.

'The place looks great, doesn't it?' I said as we hugged and exchanged cheery hellos. Adam had arrived back at the Mills farm as the fire brigade were damping it down. The sheer terror on his face evaporated when he spotted Lizzie safe and well.

We'd all suffered scary moments over the past few months, some more terrifying than others, but we'd come through it and were much stronger for it.

'When's Zak getting here?' Elizabeth asked, her voice betraying the excitement I also felt at my brother being invited to the grand opening of a new Hood Academy.

'They should be here soon. Cody dropped me off and went to park the car.'

I never thought I'd be talking about the local werewolf pack's arrival at a hunters' academy, but a new head, and a new oath were only a few of the changes being made this year.

Miss Ross and Sebastian had approached the GA with their proposal to work with the local wolf community to build a better understanding of each other's roles in society. It was groundbreaking stuff, and we were all eager to be a part of it.

I spotted Sebastian through the crowd and waved him over to where we'd found a small space to stand at the side of the room.

'Welcome back to Hood Academy,' Sebastian said beaming at us in turn. 'Let's hope this academic year is a bit quieter than the last.' He winked at me, and I couldn't help but laugh. It certainly had been a whirlwind year with many transformations.

I pulled him to one side so that we could talk privately. So much had happened recently and I hadn't had a chance to tell him that Parker was guilty of my mother's death. Sebastian had held himself accountable for too long.

'I owe you an apology,' I said, suddenly feeling nervous. 'I blamed you for Mum's death and now I know that wasn't the truth. It was Parker.'

Sebastian leaned forward and took my hands in his. 'I know it was. I read his notes in the file you took from his office.'

'Why didn't you say anything? You let me carry on thinking you were responsible.'

He smiled at me and his eyes lit up. 'You were dealing with enough without having to think about me and your mother, Mia. After Ethan injected you I spent hours at your side trying everything to save you. Cody told me what the two of you had overheard and I realised that was the trigger that forced your full shift to werewolf. I couldn't spare you the anguish and pain of turning, but I most definitely wanted to save you from further despair.'

'So you would have allowed me to think the worst of you to keep me safe?'

'Always,' he said softly.

It was at that moment I realised how far we'd come as father and daughter. He had lost the love of his life, and very nearly lost his only daughter, but instead he'd shown a strength of character that made me proud to call him family.

It wasn't only me he was helping either. With the destruction of the Mills farm, Sebastian had offered his cottage to Zak and the pack. He had moved into rooms on the third floor of the academy so he could stay close to his work.

We had all found our way in the end. Elizabeth and I were due to return to our old dorm room. Lizzie wanted to continue with her studies but Miss Ross had other plans for me. With my personal knowledge of being a hybrid, and the realisation that it wasn't as rare as we first thought, I'd been offered a position as a tutor. I was in the process of developing a new course about the history of the hybrid and the talents we possess to share with the students.

A hush fell over the room as Miss Ross called for attention.

'I'd like to ask all the students to make their way through to the library, so please take your places as quickly as you can, and we'll begin.'

We followed the crowd and spilled out into the library. The shelves had been pushed to the sides of the room, and hundreds of folding chairs filled every inch of the thick burgundy carpet except for a walkway through the centre.

We took our place on the front line where Miss Ross had put reserved signs on a row of seats. My skin tingled, and my stomach fluttered when I thought about the future. Not only the future of Hood Academy and its students, but my own outlook. I was a hybrid: half hunter and half wolf. I could do things that neither hunters nor wolves could do. My skills were unique, and I took a tremendous amount of pride in being different.

Miss Ross and Sebastian stood on a raised platform at the front of the room and addressed the group.

'Welcome to Hood Academy, everyone. It's a joy to see so many of you here.' Miss Ross's voice was clear and strong, and I glanced around at the shiny faces of the new students as they hung on her every word. They'd heard the stories of the war between hunters and wolves, and the sickening way the old headmaster, Parker, had used the students as weapons.

They'd also listened to the stories of hunters and wolves working together, of students lost in the woods and being rescued by the packs, the tales of wolves standing over students to keep them warm until help arrived, and the aid given to wolves by the girls who helped Miss Ross in the hospital that night.

Good overcame evil. Darkness turned to light. Miss Ross knew how to capture the imagination of these girls and mould them into honest, caring, and tolerant human beings.

'It's my pleasure to introduce a special guest to you all today. Someone who is a large part of this community and who has been a tireless friend to both Sebastian and me, and a champion for this school. May I present Zak Roberts, alpha of the Ravenshood pack.'

I felt the air leave the room as the students turned in their seats and sucked in a collective breath, watching the alpha pad down the red carpet. Zak had chosen to attend in his wolf form so that he could show the girls what they were up against if they decided to follow the old ways.

He was as big as a horse, his powerful limbs visible beneath his glossy fur. He looked magnificent, and I savoured the lightness in my chest as I watched my brother mount the platform and stand beside Sebastian.

The students remained silent as Miss Ross cleared her throat, none of them taking their eyes off Zak.

'I'd also like to introduce a few other members of Zak's pack. Gentlemen, if you could join us here for a moment.' She motioned for Cody, Terry, and Byron, who bashfully inched out of their seats and strode to the front.

Terry grinned at the young girls in the front row, and I watched the red flush touch their cheeks in turn at his attention. Elizabeth giggled at my side too, and I rolled my eyes at her. Only Terry could manage to get half the school crushing on him.

'These young men helped to secure the future of Hood Academy and the hunters' oath. They fought side by side with some of our most determined hunters to banish evil and bring us into the light. Can we give them a round of applause?'

The library erupted into claps and cheers as my friends waved and grinned at the audience. Elizabeth and I joined the chorus of cheers and laughed as they each took a bow in turn.

Once the noise had died down Miss Ross winked at me from the stage.

'Finally, I'd like to present to you one of our newest tutors, an ex-student, and a unique young woman. Mia, will you join me?'

Elizabeth squeezed my fingers as I stood and I felt her strength mesh with my own as I faced the sea of expectant faces. They seemed so young, and yet they were only a year or two younger than me. I'd turned seventeen during the weeks we spent destroying the Evermore warehouses and saving our friends. I'd registered the day but didn't tell anyone. At the time it wasn't important, but now I knew it had marked a new beginning for me.

'Thanks, Miss Ross.' I smiled across at my godmother, and she nodded. She knew I was ready to face the future and embrace who I was and I was grateful for her continued guidance. 'I'm here to share something very special with you all. Something that will cement the future of this academy and give us all something to fight for. Standing together makes us stronger, and we can learn so much from one another. Zak is—' I swept my hand out towards the alpha, who held his head high as he watched me speak. 'Zak is not only a fierce and loyal alpha, but he is also my brother.'

There was a rippling of whispers from the students.

'Cody isn't just another member of Zak's pack, he's my boyfriend. Miss Ross is my godmother as well as my headmis-

SHELLEY WILSON

tress, and Dr Roberts, well, Sebastian is my father, and I am proud of each and every one of them. We have been through so much together, but we're still here standing shoulder to shoulder, and that's a beautiful thing.'

There were tears in Elizabeth's eyes as I glanced over at my friend. Adam smiled up at me with a fire in his eyes that told me he was as much a member of my pack as everyone else. Cody, Terry, and Byron beamed at me from their seats, and near the back of the room, I caught the twirl of a pigtail as Ari bounced up and down in her seat.

History had been made today, and we were all a part of it. I felt the warmth of Zak's fur as he moved to stand beside me and the touch of a cool hand slip into mine as Sebastian stood on my other side.

'I'm so proud of you, Mia.'

I smiled up at the man who had saved me, even if I hadn't known it at the time. I smiled at the man who had loved my mother unconditionally, and I smiled at the man he would become. 'Thanks, Dad,' I whispered.

I turned back to the assembled group and cleared my throat. 'I'd like to share the hunters' oath with you.'

As one, the students stood up and placed their hands on their chest. They waited eagerly for me to recite the words and invite them into the community. I'd never felt so proud in my life. Finally, I knew where I belonged, and I knew who I was, and as I glanced over at my friends, family, and pack, I knew I was home.

'To every pack, a cub is born, and every hunter gets their dawn. Nurturing friendships that grow deeper, united together as an Oath Keeper.'

ACKNOWLEDGMENTS

Thank you first and foremost to my parents for their unwavering support of everything I produce. Mum, you are the best saleswoman in the world. Thank you.

Thank you to my daughter's friend, Elizabeth, for the loan of your beautiful name—I hope our Elizabeth did you proud.

A huge thank you to the team at BHC Press for working on my book and turning it into a living entity. I'm pretty sure I shall continue to squeal with delight at every cover you produce for many years to come.

Thanks to my wonderful editor, Sooz, for believing in my story, guiding me when I had my dark moments, and patiently waiting for me to emerge from the treeline.

ABOUT THE AUTHOR

Shelley Wilson's love of fantasy began at the tender age of eight when she followed Enid Blyton up a *Magical Faraway Tree*.

Inspired by Blyton's make believe world, Shelley began to create her stories, weaving tales around faeries, witches and dragons.

Writing has always been Shelley's first love, but she has also enjoyed a variety of job roles along the way; from waitressing to sales and marketing and even working as a turkey plucker.

Shelley lives in the West Midlands, UK with her three teenage children, two fish and a dragon called Roger. She is at her happiest with a slice of pizza in one hand, a latte in the other and *Game of Thrones* on the TV. She would love to live in the Shire but fears her five foot ten inch height may cause problems. She is an obsessive list writer, huge social media addict and a full-time day dreamer.

www.shelleywilsonauthor.co.uk
www.bhcpress.com

Lightning Source UK Ltd.
Milton Keynes UK
UKHW041813281118
333115UK00001B/7/P